Dear Reader,

I've always known what I've wanted in a woman, and—with a little bit of finesse and great attention to detail—I've always gotten what I wanted. The feeling's been mutual, of course.

It seems like forever since I've been drawn in, mystified by a member of the opposite sex. But I have the willpower to wait until the right one comes along.

Abby Lyndon is *not* the right one. She's crazy. Impulsive. Unrestrained. She's also keeping something from me. And I'm not going to let her out of my sight until she satisfies my curiosity—and several other uncontrollable urges.

Torr Latimer

Oregon

JAYNE ANN KRENTZ

Uneasy Alliance

Oregon

Harlequin Books

TORONTO • NEW YORK • LONDON
AMSTERDAM • PARIS • SYDNEY • HAMBURG
STOCKHOLM • ATHENS • TOKYO • MILAN
MADRID • WARSAW • BUDAPEST • AUCKLAND

HARLEQUIN ENTERPRISES LTD.
225 Duncan Mill Road, Don Mills,
Ontario, Canada M3B 3K9

UNEASY ALLIANCE

ISBN: 0-373-45187-3

Published Harlequin Enterprises, Ltd. 1984, 1993, 1995

All the characters in this book have no existence outside the
imagination of the author and have no relation whatsoever to
anyone bearing the same name or names. They are not even
distantly inspired by any individual known or unknown to the
author, and all incidents are pure invention.

1

IT WAS DURING the third class in the art of Japanese flower arrangement that Torr Latimer finally permitted himself to acknowledge exactly what it was about Abby Lyndon's designs that stirred his curiosity. They made him wonder if she would bring the same impulsive, warm abandon to a man's bed that she brought to her floral creations.

More than that, he reflected wryly as he carefully added a thistle stalk to his own spare design, Abby's arrangements made him wonder about other things too: such as how she would look sitting across from him at the breakfast table the morning after he had made love to her. His instincts told him she would appear as charmingly cheerful and disarrayed as that design of ferns and jonquils she had put together the week before.

He eyed the long honey-colored hair that was loosely arranged in a topknot. The fact that she was wearing sleek black jeans and a black sweater vaguely amused him. She had worn the black leather trench coat again this evening and the entire outfit was reminiscent of military commando attire. But nothing Abby wore could camouflage the bright, vividly impulsive woman beneath. He wondered why she bothered to try.

Hell, he thought grimly. It had been too long since he'd been with a woman. But that wasn't the real problem. The real problem was that it seemed like forever since he'd actually been thoroughly drawn in, mystified by a woman. When a man was facing forty he had no excuse for not knowing the difference between a passing attraction and something far more risky. Torr knew the difference.

And to think he'd signed up for these classes in flower arrangement because the discipline and austerity of the Japanese way with flowers had appealed to his controlled, severe way of dealing with life. It had been a philosophical whim to take the course.

Who could have guessed that the most interesting aspect of the class would be the least disciplined, least austere student in the room, he asked himself. Abby Lyndon would never master the highly formal floral design if she repeated the four-week class all year long. It had first amused and then fascinated Torr to watch Abby's chaotic, blithe arrangements grow and grow until there was nothing of simplicity or moderation left. She was the despair of the instructor, Mrs. Yamamoto, but Torr found himself enthralled and recklessly captivated.

Tonight he wanted to take Abby Lyndon home and do all sorts of intriguing, foolhardy things. The realization made him strangely restless.

He eyed the exuberant design of Queen Anne's lace and daffodils taking shape under her hands as she worked industriously at the table next to his. She had exciting hands, Torr thought. Long, delicate fingers tipped with graceful, oval nails that had been painted the color of carmine tulips. He watched her add a daffodil at an unstudied angle and lifted an eyebrow in silent surprise.

There was something different about the way she was creating her arrangement tonight. Something too intent and almost desperate about the way she was stuffing the flowers into the plastic holder. If he hadn't been watching her so closely for the past few classes he might not have noticed.

Out of the corner of his eye he saw a daffodil stalk break as she stabbed it too quickly into the plastic.

"Oh, nuts." The exclamation was a hiss of disgust as Abby tossed aside the broken daffodil. Her brows drew together in a fierce frown as she contemplated the unbalanced creation in front of her. She shot a surreptitious glance at the beautifully simple design taking shape at the next table. Torr Latimer's materials never accidentally snapped or broke under his careful, precise fingers. She chewed her lip morosely as she studied his work.

He looked up as if he knew she were watching him and a cool, reserved smile curved the corner of his rather grim mouth. Everything about Torr Latimer was a bit grim, Abby decided abruptly. Perhaps that was what had been bothering her about him for the past few weeks. There was a remote, reserved aura about him that made her wary. It hinted at strength and willpower, she told herself. Not bad qualities in a man. It was just that she was always going to be careful around strong, self-willed men. She'd had enough of masculine resoluteness and aggression to last her a lifetime.

"I have some more daffodils if you'd like a replacement," Torr murmured gently in the dark, gravelly voice that always made her think of a riverbed.

"You always seem to have extra materials and I never have enough," Abby observed regretfully. "Mrs. Yamamoto says I still haven't learned restraint." She surveyed the conglomeration of daffodils and Queen Anne's lace in front of her gloomily. "It's just that my arrangements always seem to run out of control."

"They have a charm all their own."

Abby smiled in quick gratitude before frowning once more at her flowers. "That's very kind of you, but it should be obvious by now that I don't seem to be getting the hang of this particular style of floral design. You're a natural at it, though. How can you resist the temptation to add more and more materials?"

Torr shrugged, his eyes on the elegantly simple and vital design he had created. "Perhaps I'm just not as naturally adventurous as you are. Do you want another daffodil?" He picked one up from the small pile of floral materials on his table and extended it to her.

Abby looked at the flower lying across his palm and experienced an unexpected wave of curiosity and uneasiness. The hand that held the flower was a strong square one, capable of crushing far more than a daffodil. But the flower appeared quite at home and protected by the blunt fingers. Why did she hesitate to take it from him?

Annoyed with herself for the odd reluctance, Abby reached out quickly and snapped the small gift from Torr. As she did so, she found herself meeting his remote amber gaze. It wasn't the first time she had met his eyes but the small confrontations didn't get any less disturbing with repetition. That grim watchful expression aroused her sense of caution at the same time as it fascinated her. Abby wondered what secrets lay at the bottom of the intelligent amber pools. A man like this would have a few secrets.

She was getting fanciful, she chided herself angrily. Her own little secret was probably making her over-sensitive to nonexistent secrets in others.

"Thanks," she said. As she turned back to her arrangement, she continued with a determined chattiness, "I'm sure Mrs. Yamamoto will say the last thing I need is another daffodil in this thing, but it seems to me it's just crying out for one extra bit of yellow. What do you think?"

"What you do with flowers looks like you," he said calmly. "And therefore I'm inclined to give it what you think it needs. By all means, add some more yellow."

"Very diplomatic," Abby shot back dryly as she eyed her design, wondering where to position the daffodil. "You know very well Mrs. Yamamoto is going to shake her head over my creation and then tell the whole class that you've created another masterpiece!"

He shrugged, not bothering to deny the remark. They both knew it was true. "Mrs. Yamamoto understands and appreciates discipline and restraint. She's naturally going to be biased in favor of my arrangements."

Abby's mouth curved wryly. "Meaning I lack those things?"

"Perhaps. I think I envy you."

She glanced up, surprised. "You're serious, aren't you?" She shook her head quickly as if to negate the question. "Scratch that. Of course you're serious. You're always serious."

"You seem to understand me rather well," he said ruefully.

"I've been watching you work with flowers for three weeks now," Abby said, smiling. "I suppose I've learned something about you."

"Really?" He looked genuinely intrigued. "What have you learned?"

Across the busy classroom Mrs. Yamamoto was occupied with other students. It was obvious to Abby that the instructor wasn't going to appear out of nowhere to provide an opportune interruption. Abby was going to be stuck answering the question she had elicited. Torr was watching her with a cool expectancy that made it impossible to retreat. How had she gotten herself into this?

"Oh, not all that much, to tell you the truth. I was just being a bit flippant. Don't take me seriously."

"As you've already pointed out, it's impossible for me to take things any other way. Tell me what you think you've learned about me, Abby."

"Fortune-tellers get paid good money for this kind of work, you know!"

"I'll pay you."

"For heaven's sake!" she exclaimed, startled at the deliberate way he said that. "I was only kidding. Look, I really haven't learned all that much about you. It's just that I get the impression you're, well, rather cautious and conservative about life in general. You probably don't take a lot of senseless risks or go crazy on weekends or do wild, undisciplined things. That's all." He was just like his designs, she thought privately. Concentrated, elegant, restrained. But darned if she was going to say that part aloud!

Torr nodded his head as she rattled off her description. His black hair with its faint trace of gray suited the dark, controlled strength she sensed in him, Abby thought. The thickness of the black lashes, which framed the amber eyes, were the only soft touches amid the harsh angles and planes of his face. He was dressed, as he usually was, in a manner as reserved and dark as his personality. A conservatively cut shirt in a somber pattern of dense gray and indigo stripes, and a pair of expensive well-cut gray trousers outlined a solidly built, utterly masculine body.

He would crush a woman in bed, Abby found herself thinking suddenly and then knew a fierce, highly uncomfortable awareness as her imagination insisted on visualizing what it would be like to be the woman Torr Latimer overwhelmed in bed. Good grief! What was the matter with her? She had more than enough problems of her own tonight without indulging in flights of erotic fantasy.

Beneath her agitated fingers, the daffodil snapped.

She sighed and said, "Mrs. Yamamoto is probably going to kick me out of class."

Torr watched her curiously as she hastily deposited the second broken daffodil into a brown paper bag, the same bag into which she had stuffed the first. "Do you think you can hide the remains that way? Mrs. Yamamoto is the kind of instructor who can account for every missing daffodil."

"I know and now I've got two bodies in the bag," Abby replied. "Oh, well, there's only one more class session. She probably won't do anything more drastic than shake her head in that sad little way she has. I think she's accepted the fact that I'm not going to make it big in the art of Japanese flower arrangement. I heard her encouraging you to show one of your designs at the festival next month, though. Going to do it?"

"No."

Abby stared at him. "Of course you are. How could you refuse? Your work is fantastic," she went on with impulsive warmth. "Mrs. Yamamoto wouldn't be encouraging you if she didn't think you'd do very well."

"I'm just not interested, I suppose. I took the class more out of curiosity than anything else. I don't intend to take up flower arranging as a full-time hobby."

Abby's shock was reflected in her blue eyes. "That's ridiculous. How can you say that? Why should you turn your back on something you do so well? You have a talent and I refuse to let you ignore it."

His expression of sardonic inquiry made her realize how recklessly she had spoken. It certainly wasn't any of her business whether or not he pursued his flower-arranging skills. She ought to have learned by now that her natural streak of impulsiveness was not one of her greatest virtues.

"You're going to refuse to let me ignore it?" Torr queried interestedly, as if the notion of another person telling him what he could or could not do was entirely new to him.

"It would crush Mrs. Yamamoto if you didn't enter the competition," Abby pointed out.

"She'll survive." He waited, clearly expecting further arguments.

"You'd probably get a lot of personal satisfaction out of winning a prize for your talents," she added brightly.

"I doubt it." He continued to wait.

The fact that he fully anticipated another push from her annoyed Abby. That waiting, patient quality in him could be unsettling. He was probably just giving her a chance to try dictating to him so that he could smoothly squash the small act of feminine tyranny. Something told her that Torr Latimer was not the kind of man any woman would ever successfully dominate. But the acceptance of his obvious strength of will was not nearly as intimidating as it probably should have been. Try as she might, it was difficult remaining wary of the man. It was more fun to tease him.

Her rashness was going to get her into a great deal of trouble someday, Abby told herself and then promptly forgot the warning, just as she always did. Her mood turned to one of mischief.

"I have an idea. Why don't you design the arrangement and I'll enter it under my name?"

"You'd cheat?" He didn't sound disapproving, merely intrigued.

"Oh, for pity's sake. You really don't have much of a sense of humor, do you? It was a joke."

"I'm sorry. I'm a little slow on the uptake sometimes."

She cast him a disparaging glance. "Don't try the humble, self-effacing bit with me," she advised heartily. "I know very well you're not at all slow on the up-take. You're just more interested in the subtle than in the obvious."

"Something else you've learned from watching me design flower arrangements?"

"I suppose so."

There was a pause. "Abby, I know you came to class on the bus tonight. Will you allow me to drive you home?"

Abby blinked, startled. For a split second she let herself think about how pleasant it would be to have this strong, solid man beside her tonight when she opened the door of her downtown apartment. Then she pushed the thought aside. She was not going to let herself succumb to fantasy!

"That's very kind of you, but I . . ."

"Abby, kindness really doesn't enter into this. I'd like to take you home."

"It's thoughtful of you, but I don't need . . ."

"Are you nervous about me, Abby?" He sounded genuinely concerned.

"Of course not! Who could be nervous about a man who takes Japanese flower-arrangement classes?" Abby shot back bracingly, just as Mrs. Yamamoto material-ized beside her with a distressed frown on her pleasant middle-aged face. Instantly Abby turned her full at-tention to apologizing for the out-of-control design of daffodils and Queen Anne's lace.

"I know, Mrs. Yamamoto," she began hurriedly, aware that Torr was listening quietly as he lounged against his own worktable. "I went crazy again. I just couldn't seem to get it balanced. I kept adding more bits and pieces of leaves and flowers and things, thinking I could sort of even up the overall design, but it ran away from me as usual."

"Abby," the older woman sighed, "you should have stopped a dozen daffodils ago. Look at this. It wanders all over the place. I thought that perhaps working alongside Mr. Latimer might help you control your impulsive design streak. Just look at how he limits himself to the barest essentials to convey the feeling of harmony and proportion." Mrs. Yamamoto turned toward Torr's design with pleasure and deep approval.

As the diminutive instructor moved to admire her star pupil's handiwork, Abby met Torr's eyes over Mrs. Yamamoto's head. Her sense of humor rose to the surface and unthinkingly she made a face at him—a perfect ten-year-old's grimace.

"Teacher's pet," she mouthed silently and knew he had caught the words just as he politely turned to discuss his creation with the other woman.

"You'll be pleased to know, Mrs. Yamamoto," Torr said smoothly, "that Abby has decided to let me give her some outside instruction this evening after class. I'm hoping that working on a one-to-one basis I may be able to explain some of the basic principles more clearly to her."

"Excellent." The instructor approved with a gentle nod. "You will make a very good teacher for her. All she needs is a little guidance and discipline."

Abby rolled her eyes beseechingly toward heaven as Torr nodded seriously.

"I'll do my best," he said.

Forty minutes later Abby found herself seated in Torr Latimer's gray BMW, her mood hovering between amusement and exasperation.

"Guidance and discipline," she mocked reproachfully. "Honestly, Torr, even you can't be serious about trying to teach me the fine art of Japanese flower arrangement! I don't know why I let you talk me into taking me home tonight. The bus would have been just fine."

"I wanted to take you home," he said simply, slanting her a quick glance as he piloted the car sedately through the drizzly April Oregon night. "Besides, it's raining."

"It does that a lot here in Portland in case you haven't noticed."

"I've noticed," he countered.

"You say that as if you're a native," she said, smiling.

"No. I've only lived here for about three years." The words held a certain crispness, as if further questions in that direction would not be welcomed. Perhaps he wasn't the type to want to waste time discussing what he considered trivial matters, Abby decided. She began to wonder what one did discuss with a fellow flower-arranging student.

"Nice car," she tried brightly. "I've always wanted to buy a foreign car. But one has to worry so much about getting them properly serviced." She decided not to add that if she had been able to buy such a car it would have been something a bit more dashing than a BMW—say a Jaguar or a Lotus. But this car seemed to fit the man: solid, well-built, durable and tough.

"It's okay, Abby," Torr responded in quiet amusement, "you said yourself that you could hardly be nervous around a man you met in a class on flower design, remember?"

"I'm not nervous. But I guess I am a little curious about why you wanted to take me home tonight."

"Because you're like the flower arrangements you create," he told her whimsically.

She shot him a sharp glance. "Is this where I get my free analysis?"

"If you like."

She tilted her head in a challenging manner. "Okay, let's hear it."

He didn't hesitate. "You're interesting, impulsive, imaginative and intriguing."

"Amazing. You have a talent for alliteration as well as flower design."

"You even look a little like the flowers we've been arranging in class," Torr went on evenly. "A waist as slender as the stem of a daffodil, hair the color of clover honey, eyes like—"

"Don't say cornflower blue," she broke in, chuckling. "I hate cornflowers."

"Gentian?" he offered politely.

Abby's chuckles turned to outright laughter. "You're grasping at straws now!"

"You're right. No point carrying analogies to extremes. Actually, your eyes are sort of a smoke blue. Very unusual."

"Well, you've hit the high points. Better stop there."

"You're not taking me seriously, are you?" he inquired softly.

"Should I?"

He nodded once, no hint of humor in the craggy lines of his bluntly unhandsome face. "Yes, I think you'd better."

Abby shifted uneasily as she caught the certainty in his voice. It occurred to her that she didn't know much about Torr Latimer except that he had a talent for flower arrangement. It also occurred to her that he seemed to occupy a large portion of the interior of the BMW. His presence in the car was almost intimidating. He wasn't quite six feet tall but there was no denying the sense of potent strength in him. Still, she *had* met him in a flower-design class, Abby reminded herself resolutely.

"I live in the apartment house on the next block. You can park in front," she said quickly, infusing her voice with brisk friendliness. She didn't want to think about whether she really reminded him of a flower. It brought disturbing images to mind of being *arranged* by him. Perhaps arranged on a bed.

The BMW was brought to a purring halt beside a parking space that appeared much too small to Abby's eyes. She experienced a sense of relief at the thought that if he couldn't find a place to park on the street, Torr might simply be forced to let her out on the sidewalk and take himself home.

But the BMW fit into the tiny slot as if the car had been designed for it and Abby stifled a small sigh. Now he would walk her to her door. She was sure of it. Then what?

"Would you care for a cup of tea?" she heard herself ask weakly as he guided her through the main door and into the elevator of the handsome brick building. The apartment house had been built during the first half of the century, but it had been meticulously restored and it retained the spacious, high-ceilinged rooms that had been part of the original design. Abby's apartment was a comfortable one-bedroom plan on the fifth floor with a large kitchen and oversize windows to let in plenty of light.

"Tea might be a bit much on top of an evening of flowers and art," Torr said calmly. "Have you got anything stronger?"

"Well, yes, there's some cognac—"

"That will be fine," he interrupted positively, as they stepped from the elevator. Taking the key from her hand as they paused in the hallway outside her apartment, he opened the door with a cool familiarity that somehow managed to disturb her again. What was it about this man that kept sending mixed signals? One moment she was certain he was reassuringly polite and manageable; the next she was reacting with an almost primitive disquiet to his presence.

"I'll get the cognac," she said quickly as she stepped through the doorway into the eclectically furnished room. The cheerful vanilla-and-papaya color scheme, underscored with accents of black, reflected Abby's love of light airy colors and her occasional taste for pure drama. The overall effect of the style would have been one of witty sophistication if it hadn't been for the stacks of boxes standing in the hall, piled in every corner of the living room and filling the closet just inside the door.

"What the . . . ?" Torr's muttered exclamation of surprise came as he accidentally struck one of the boxes with the toe of his Italian leather shoe.

"Sorry about that," Abby said, stooping down hastily to shove the pile of boxes to one side. "It's just that I'm rather short of storage space, you see."

"What's in them?" Curiously he glanced around at the endless stacks of boxes.

"Vitamins," she said succinctly, discarding her gutsy black leather trench coat. Abby had always liked the coat. She felt it gave her a certain bold cachet. The kind of casual aggressiveness that warned men not to try to encroach on her private space. Unfortunately, as far as she could tell, Torr hadn't appeared to notice this statement of hers. Maybe it was because he came by a state of quiet assertiveness so naturally. Ah, well, perhaps the coat wasn't the most effective method of making such statements, Abby decided. After all, she'd bought it the way she'd bought most of her clothes: impulsively.

"Vitamins?" Torr picked up one of the green-and-gold boxes and examined the label. "You must take a lot of them. 'MegaLife Vitamin Supplements, for the person who insists on living life to the fullest extent,'" he read. "You must live a very full life, judging by the thousands of vitamins stored in this room."

"Don't be ridiculous. Even I couldn't take this many vitamins. I sell them. Or rather I distribute them to people who sell them for me. Door to door." In the kitchen Abby located the cognac bottle and pulled it down from the cupboard. "It's amazing what people will buy on impulse when you show up at their door with a well-designed display."

"I would imagine you'd be fairly good at understanding impulse buying," Torr remarked behind her.

"Was that a nasty crack?" she demanded suspiciously.

"No, a joke. A poor one. It would appear that the business is a thriving one," he added with innocent interest.

"Very," she informed him dryly. "What's more, I believe in my own product." She poured him a glass of cognac and then reached for a green-and-gold bottle sitting on the counter. Casually she unscrewed the top and popped two of the tablets into her mouth.

"What's that?"

"B complex and vitamin C. Good for stress." She resealed the jar, her mouth full of vitamins, and poured herself a glass of cognac. She downed the tablets with an overlarge swallow of the potent brandy and wound up trying to stifle a choking cough.

"Water might have been more effective than cognac," Torr observed as he politely stepped forward and thumped her between the shoulder blades.

"Thank you," she gasped unevenly. "I, uh, was just trying to save a little time."

"Are we in a hurry?" he asked mildly.

"Well, no, I guess not. I tend to cut corners occasionally. Shall we go into the living room?" she added with determined politeness. How embarrassing. She should have taken the time to run a glass of water.

"Why are you taking tablets for stress? Are you under a great deal?" Torr asked pleasantly.

"Isn't everyone these days?" she retorted, wishing she'd kept her mouth shut. Taking a seat on the papaya-colored sofa, she waved him airily to the black armchair. It was time to take a firmer grip on the conversation. "What about you, Torr? What do you do when you're not arranging flowers?" There, that sounded casual and brisk.

"I buy and sell," he said quietly.

She arched an eyebrow. "What do you buy and sell?"

"Stress." He smiled faintly as if surprised to realize he might have made a small joke.

"You'll have to be a bit more explicit, I'm afraid. I'm not big on subtlety, remember?" Abby said crisply.

"Sorry. It wasn't really all that subtle or clever. I only meant that in a sense I deal in other people's stress. I buy and sell commodities futures."

Abby's eyes opened very wide. "Like pork bellies?"

He permitted himself another small smile. "And gold and wheat and corn and several other products. I made the remark about dealing in stress because so much of the buying and selling that goes on is done under great stress. People panic, people despair, people get far too excited. In short, they often go nuts buying and selling commodities. Lots of stress."

"Sounds like a good market for me. Want to buy some vitamins?" Abby asked hopefully.

Torr shook his head. "I'm afraid I don't have much use for them."

"No ulcers? No hypertension?"

"No."

"You don't fall victim to all this buying-and-selling stress?" she demanded dubiously.

"No."

"Why not, if it's so common?"

He hesitated, lifting his amber eyes to meet hers in one of the direct, disturbing glances she was coming to dread. "Possibly because I don't get excited about the action. It's just a way to make a living. I'm good at it, but I don't get emotionally involved the way so many people do."

"Mr. Cool, hmmm? Well," she began in her best sales tone, "it just so happens that MegaLife makes a basic, high-potency formula that is designed to meet all the daily needs of the cool, healthy male in his forties—"

"In that case, I've got a year's grace before I have to start in on them," Torr interrupted calmly.

"Oh, sorry. You're not forty?"

"Next year." He sipped his cognac, not appearing unduly upset by her assumption of his age. "What about you, Abby? Which daily formula are you taking?"

"The one for the healthy female in her thirties," Abby replied, sighing.

"I would have said you'd need the one for the woman in her twenties."

"Thanks." She grimaced. "Actually, I'm twenty-nine but I decided to advance to the higher potency formula a year early."

"Plus a few supplements such as that B complex you downed out there in the kitchen?"

"Can't be too careful. Now that we've exhausted that topic, what would you like to discuss?" She gave him a bright, aloofly inquiring glance as she took a sip of her cognac. It was getting late and she was beginning to wonder how she was going to get rid of Torr Latimer. He didn't show any signs of finishing his drink and making a polite exit.

"Us."

Abby choked on her cognac and Torr got to his feet in concern as she began to cough. An instant later she felt a solid thump on her back that nearly sent her sprawling across the smoked-glass coffee table.

"Are you all right?" he asked, his hand in readiness to strike again.

"Yes, yes, I'm fine, thank you!" she gasped, battling to regain her breath and her equilibrium. "Uh, Torr...Mr. Latimer, it's getting awfully late. Don't you think you'd better be heading home? I know you com- modities people must get up very early. The markets are back East, aren't they?"

"Tomorrow's Saturday. The market's closed on Sat- urday."

"Oh." She frantically searched her brain for another excuse.

"Abby, I'm sorry if I disconcerted you," he said gent- ly as he sat down again in the black armchair and reached for his cognac. His face was set in a faint frown and his eyes watched her with the intensity of a hawk.

"Torr," she said, grabbing for her self-control, "I think this is a very good time to tell you that I'm not looking for a relationship of any kind at the moment. My life is very busy just now. I have my business to at- tend to and . . . and several other matters of a personal nature that I won't bore you with. If you're thinking of suggesting that we, uh, become involved, then I'm afraid I must regretfully decline."

"Regretfully decline?" There was a sudden trace of something that might have passed for humor in his amber eyes.

"That did sound a bit stilted, didn't it?" she admitted.

"It sounded as if you were turning down a formal invitation to a garden party."

"I'm sorry. Frankly, you've caught me off guard. I really do have a lot of things on my mind tonight."

"I'm not inviting you to a garden party, Abby. I was about to invite you to bed."

Abby closed her eyes and tried again to catch her breath. This man had a way of knocking it out of her, even when he didn't lay a hand on her. "Since you insist on being very forthright about your invitation, then I will try to show you the same courtesy," she finally managed icily. Regally she got to her feet. The jeans and black sweater she was wearing didn't detract a bit from the cool, dismissive air she was attempting to project. "The answer is no. Good night, Torr."

He watched her a moment longer as if debating his next move. Then he too got to his feet, a strangely rueful expression on his face.

"I rushed that a bit, didn't I? Not like me, really. I'm usually rather slow and cautious. Especially when I'm dealing with a particularly fragile sort of flower. Abby, I won't push you. But I'd like us to be clear about our relationship and where it's going. Right from the start. Things will be simpler that way."

"Simpler?" she uttered, unable to collect her thoughts. His heavy strength was intimidating on some levels, but oddly alluring on others. She must be out of her mind to be fascinated with this man. She ought to be sending him home at once in his elegantly staid foreign car. She should never have allowed him to drive her home in the first place.

"I didn't get a chance to finish telling you all the ways you remind me of a flower," Torr went on huskily, moving closer, putting out a large hand to gently cup the nape of her neck.

"Torr..."

"I told you that your waist was as slim as the stem of a daffodil," he murmured, lowering his head to her throat. "But I didn't get around to explaining that your breasts make me think of two very delicate, very luscious orchids."

Abby felt his strong fingers skim lightly down the front of her black sweater, seeking the shape of her small rounded breasts. This was where she should be getting nervous, she told herself. She was a fool not to push him away. Or was it even possible to push a rock of Torr's size and density?

That thought caught at her imagination and her fingertips came up to shove almost experimentally at his broad chest. Nothing happened. He didn't appear to even notice the cautious, testing push she gave him.

Abby drew in her breath and waited for the uncertainty and the hint of fear that ought to be materializing in her brain. Neither came.

She had a few seconds to realize that the tendrils of flickering emotion curling deep in her body were not the first questing thrusts of fear but of an unfamiliar excitement, and then she felt Torr's hands gliding down to her waist and over the contours of her hips.

Torr uttered a deep, thick groan as he found the curves of her lower body. "And your sweet, soft little rear makes me think of a gladiolus."

"Not a Venus's-flytrap?" Abby managed tartly as she struggled to find a way to deal with a situation that she sensed could easily get out of control.

"Never," he vowed and then his mouth moved up along the line of her throat to hover just above her uncertainly parted lips. "I've been aching to taste you all evening." His lips closed on hers with an urgency and a hunger that Abby realized instantly were only just held in check. The thought that this man, who seemed in such possession of himself, wanted her this much was unsettling and intoxicating.

There was no cautious sampling of the nectar he clearly expected to find. Instead, just as Abby had distantly sensed earlier that evening, Torr Latimer overwhelmed and claimed her mouth as if it were his by right. Abby knew that if she had been lying beneath him instead of standing on her feet she would have been crushed exactly as she had imagined.

What shook her was that the prospect didn't hold the fear it should have held.

She felt his hands slide heavily down her back again to cup the curves of her derriere and then he used the intimate grip to urge her against his thighs. Abby moaned as she felt the evidence of his arousal and knew he wanted her to be aware of it.

"I've been thinking about this since the first night of class. Tonight I decided I couldn't wait any longer. You intrigue me so, sweet Abby. You make me want you.

And it's been so long. . . ." The words disappeared into her mouth as he thrust his tongue deeply inside.

If that was all this was about, Abby decided in sudden anxiety, she would end it now. If Torr Latimer had simply been so long without a woman that any woman would do, she was certainly not going to be accommodating. The thought gave her the strength to push much more fiercely against his broad shoulders.

He didn't release her, but one of his hands moved to soothe the back of her neck, holding her with gentle firmness as she attempted to wrench free her mouth.

Still there was no fear, only the unexpected tantalizing excitement. Abby could feel it pulsing through her now, knew that Torr undoubtedly sensed it. She trembled against him and he muttered something that sounded very male and very satisfied. Then slowly, with a reluctance that left her mouth damp and tremulous, he raised his head.

His amber eyes were flaring with the force of his desire and Abby saw the deep intent at the bottom of the golden pools. Her body throbbed with the sensual awareness he had created and her mind spun with unasked questions and an unnamed need. Both the awareness and the need were so foreign that she didn't want to bring herself to face them directly. Everything was moving much too fast.

And then everything came to a screeching halt with Torr's next words.

"Abby, honey, I have to know now if there's anyone else. Are you free to be with me tonight? Is there any other man in your life? *Tell me!*"

For the first time since she had let him into her apartment, her initial tendrils of uncertainty were colored with the fear that had been strangely absent. "What are you asking, Torr?" she whispered.

"You know what I'm asking. I'm not nearly as subtle as you seem to think," he ground out as his hand moved through her honey-shaded hair and dislodged the loose knot that held it at the back of her head. The thick mass tumbled to her shoulders and he watched with fascination. "Just tell me the truth, Abby. That's all I ask. I won't share you."

"Nobody asked you to share me! Torr, my private life is my business. I do not make explanations to anyone, least of all to a man I barely know."

"I'm not involved with anyone else," he said simply.

Abby's blue eyes narrowed as she looked up at him. "What's that supposed to mean?"

"That I'm being honest with you. I'm free to be here with you. All I ask is the same assurance in return. Do you belong to another man?"

She felt caught, trapped by the apparent desire for honesty, which she could not fault, yet made uneasy by the implicit possessiveness that lay buried in his question. Ultimately it was pride that governed her answer—pride and innate self-defense.

"Torr, I do not belong to any man." She saw the satisfaction move deep in his eyes and continued quickly, "And I want it made very clear that I'm not interested in belonging to a man. I'm accountable only to myself."

"As long as you're free now, I'm willing to wait to discuss the rest of the matter," he murmured. His mouth curved faintly as his thumb worked along the side of her jaw.

"Then you will wait a very long time," she snapped. He released her as she twisted out of his arms, but his eyes followed her every movement. She occupied herself by picking up the empty cognac glasses and carrying them into the kitchen. Tidying up gave her an excuse to stay out of his reach.

He followed her, coming to stand in the kitchen doorway. His dark grim presence fed her unfolding anxiety. She wanted him gone and the sooner the better. It had been a mistake to let him bring her home.

"Good night, Torr."

"You're afraid of me, aren't you?" he demanded wonderingly.

"Let's just say I think it's time I exercised a little caution," she retorted.

"I wouldn't hurt you."

"I only have your word on that, don't I?" she observed laconically. "It's been my experience that men are quite capable of hurting women, especially women they think they own. I have no desire to get involved with anyone right now, Torr, but if I did, it wouldn't be with a possessive man. And, frankly, I'm getting the impression you might be the possessive type."

His mouth hardened and she could see the calculating intent in him as he stood there so solidly in her doorway. "Will you tell me about it, Abby?" he finally asked quietly.

"No." She smiled icily. "It's none of your business."

"How can you say that when it's affecting what happens between you and me?"

"Good night, Torr. Thank you for the ride home."

He didn't move. "I'll see you tomorrow." It wasn't a question, it was a statement.

"I'm going to be busy tomorrow."

"Abby, you're judging me without giving me a chance. There's no need to be afraid of me."

His sureness melted some of the ice in her smile. "I don't think you realize quite how overwhelming you are, Torr."

"You weren't afraid of me in class or when I kissed you. Don't make snap judgments, Abby. Give us both some time. Let me take you out to dinner tomorrow night." He stepped forward as she started to shake her head and caught her face between his large palms with surprising gentleness. As her lips began to shape the word no, he lowered his mouth to hers and kissed the negative back into her throat.

Abby tensed, waiting for the fear to surge to the surface. But all she felt was the heavy warmth of Torr's body reaching out to cloak her. His kiss was no less forceful or enthralling than it had been the first time, but she still didn't respond with outright tension or anxiety. Instead, she realized wryly, she merely responded. Period.

The sensation was captivating.

"Dinner?" he whispered urgently, his mouth poised just above hers. "Please?"

"I . . ."

"Please, Abby."

She closed her eyes and did a quick rundown of all the reasons why she shouldn't and then she heard herself saying hesitantly, "All right, Torr. Dinner. Nothing else."

"Thank you." The gratitude in his deep voice made her feel awkward, as if she had overreacted. "I'll pick you up at seven. We'll go to that new place downtown near the Benson."

She nodded, not knowing what else to say as he named the new continental restaurant that had just opened near the landmark hotel in Portland.

"Good night, Abby," he said softly.

"Good night, Torr."

He dropped his hands from her and she felt cool. It made her realize how enveloped she had been by the warmth of his body when he had been standing close. Without a word he turned to go and then his gaze fell on a colorful brochure lying on the kitchen counter.

Abby bit her lip as he picked up the pamphlet advertising a resort on the Oregon coast.

"Planning a vacation?" he asked mildly.

"No!" she answered quickly, too quickly. "No, I stayed there for a weekend a couple of months ago. They sent out some advertising, I guess, and I was on their mailing list."

"You went to the coast during the winter?"

"It's very lovely in winter," she told him flatly.

"I agree," he nodded, dropping the brochure back on the counter. "Perhaps we—" He snapped off the words quickly, apparently realizing he was about to go too far. "I'll see you tomorrow evening at seven, Abby."

"Yes." Abby stared at the brochure as it fell from his fingers. "At seven."

She locked the door very carefully behind him and then she went back into the kitchen and picked up the brochure. The Misty Inn. Enjoy the spectacular Oregon coast at any season. Open all year round, the pamphlet advised cheerfully.

With grim care Abby tore it in several tiny pieces. It would be a long time before she returned to the Misty Inn. Probably never. She stuffed the pieces into a trash can under the sink.

The only logical explanation for that advertisement arriving in her mail this afternoon was that the resort was sending out such brochures to all former guests.

But even as she gave herself that argument for the thousandth time since the mail had arrived, Abby knew a sense of dread. She had been pushing it to the back of her mind all evening, but now it emerged to haunt her.

She would have felt far more certain of her conviction if the brochure had been contained in an envelope carrying the letterhead of the resort. But it hadn't. The pamphlet had been stuffed into a plain white envelope and addressed on a typewriter. There was no return address of any kind.

As she undressed for bed, Abby's thoughts were chaotic, torn between images of a strong, intense man who signed up for classes in Japanese flower arrangement and memories of a weekend in winter that she wanted desperately to forget.

2

SHE HAD ACCUSED HIM of appreciating subtlety but in truth he had been anything but subtle this evening. As a result he'd nearly ruined everything. Hell, Torr thought a little savagely as he guided the BMW up the winding hillside overlooking Portland. You'd think a man his age would have developed a bit of finesse when it came to handling a woman he wanted.

Actually, he realized, he wasn't altogether certain why he had so completely abandoned his normal restraint. But something had happened to him tonight when he'd finally acknowledged that he wanted Abby Lyndon. It was as if, having accepted the inevitable, he had simply decided to grab it with both hands.

He'd been a fool, no doubt about it. He should have taken everything much more slowly. Well, he'd been able to recover enough ground to salvage another date. That was something, at least, he told himself derisively. But he was very lucky she hadn't panicked altogether. What had made her so nervous of him, he wondered. She'd been quite friendly in class.

It had something to do with his need to be certain she was free. It was after he'd asked the crucial question that she'd really begun to withdraw. Perhaps it was because she wasn't altogether free.

Had she spent that weekend on the coast alone two months ago? Maybe she had just terminated a relationship and that was the reason she was fearful of plunging directly into another affair.

The questions spun around his head as he drove with automatic precision. The houses perched on the hillside on either side of the road appeared cozy and welcoming, their windows warm with lights. His own was going to be dark. Torr hadn't bothered to leave a light on to welcome himself home.

One thing was for certain, he reassured himself. She couldn't know enough about his past to be really afraid of him. Not yet. Not ever, if he had his way. It was something else that was disturbing her. Had something he said reminded her of another man? The one she'd gone to the coast with two months before?

His blunt fingers stretched and then gripped the wheel with a force that Torr didn't even notice. He would like very much to get his hands on the man who had made Abby so wary.

IT WAS THE mixed signals she was getting from him that were making it difficult to deal with Torr Latimer, Abby concluded the next evening as she dressed for their date. The impression of strength, for example, was at once reassuring and intimidating. She experienced an instinctive sensation of being protected by it on the one hand, while on the other, her past had taught her to be distrustful of physical strength.

If he hadn't started making demands, asking about the other men in her life, wanting to know if she was free, she might have found herself letting the kiss go

much further than it had. Abby faced the reality of that
as she slipped the sleek, body-hugging knit dress over
her head.

The dress, a silvery blue, highlighted her honey-
colored hair loosely arranged in a topknot and her blue
eyes. Not cornflower blue or gentian blue, Abby decided with a flicker of humor as she remembered Torr's
efforts to liken her to a flower the previous evening.

It had been rather flattering, actually, especially since
she didn't consider her features as a model of flower-
like beauty. The wide blue eyes, tip-tilted nose and expressive mouth went together in a reasonably attractive
fashion, but Abby didn't kid herself that there was any
riveting beauty underlying the whole.

There was, however, a vivid animation marking her
face of which Abby remained unaware. One seldom
smiled, talked to or otherwise visited with oneself in a
mirror. Mirrors were for studying an unnaturally quiet
version of oneself. As a result the image in the mirror
remained, for Abby, at least, merely reasonably attractive. The warmth and intelligent energy that were
a fundamental part of her were usually left for others
of a discerning nature to discover. There had been men
in the past who had responded to the total effect Abby
created, but not since Flynn Randolph had she allowed
one to get close.

The night before, her response to the grimly quiet
man from the flower-arranging class had startled Abby.
It was part of the disturbingly double messages she was
trying to interpret. She frowned at herself, her brows
knitting into a severe line as she applied a coral lip-
stick. Torr Latimer was not the sort of man she would

have expected to respond to so swiftly. On the other hand, as she kept reminding herself, she had met him in a class on flower arrangement!

That thought brought a reluctant smile to her face as she turned away from the mirror to answer the demanding clamor of her doorbell. Torr was right on time, showing a promptness that didn't surprise her in the least. She had had a hunch he was the precise, punctual type.

He was also, she realized as she opened the door, every bit as unsettling and intimidating tonight as he had been the night before. The dark suit he wore was set off by a formal white shirt adorned with a conservative tie and small cuff links. Real gold cuff links, Abby noted with a flash of annoyance. Was he rich?

"Something wrong?" he asked politely as she continued to stare up at him. "Did I use the wrong knot on the tie?"

She shook her head, breaking the small spell, and stood back to let him inside. "No, of course not. I was just wondering if you were rich. Watch out for that stack of panthothenic-acid tablets. I just got a new shipment in today."

"Does it matter?" Torr avoided the uneven stack of green-and-gold boxes piled just inside the door.

"If you hit the tablets? Not to me. You're the one who'd have to pick them up and restack them," she answered, grinning wryly.

"I meant would it matter if I'm rich?" he said patiently.

"Well, I usually don't date men who might be a great deal more successful than I am," she explained honestly.

"If you like, we can compare bank balances over dinner," he murmured, amber eyes gleaming as he surveyed her slender figure in the close-fitting blue dress. "Although, I have to admit the topic doesn't sound particularly exciting."

"It might if it turned out I was a lot richer than you," she suggested blithely, moving away to collect her black leather trench coat.

"Do you think you might be?"

"No," she replied, sighing.

"You're really wary of rich men?"

"I'm cautious."

"I think you're cautious about every sort of man." He held the door for her. "Someday you'll have to tell me why."

"You haven't answered my question."

"About being rich?" He lifted one shoulder negligently as he took her arm. "That's a relative situation, don't you think? How do I know what you'd consider rich?"

She was silent as they rode the elevator downstairs and walked through the lobby. "You're not going to answer the question, are you?" she finally demanded shrewdly.

"Not now. No."

"Which means you probably are rich," she groaned.

"I asked you not to make snap judgments last night," he reminded her as he escorted her out to the waiting BMW.

"I'm not the only one who has that problem," she pointed out as he slid into the seat beside her. "You made some pretty fast judgments yourself last night."

"Deciding that I wanted to go to bed with you wasn't a snap judgment." He switched on the ignition and pulled away from the curb with efficient skill. "I'd been watching you create those wild hopelessly chaotic flower arrangements for three weeks before I realized that it was the creator of the arrangements and not the designs themselves which appealed to me."

"I'm not sure I should find that flattering." Abby's mouth lifted irrepressibly at the corners. "I mean if it took you three weeks to realize it was me instead of the flowers you wanted to date . . ."

"I tend to make my mind up slowly and carefully," he admitted.

"I thought people who traded commodities had to make quick decisions all the time."

"I made the basic decision to get into commodities only after a lot of deliberation. Once into them I was committed. The trading part is a combination of skill and luck—just like any other business. I'm relatively good at business. After the basic decision of whether or not to trade has been made, the other judgments don't require a lot of meditation. One just does what has to be done in order to be successful."

"So now I'm a business decision? I think I prefer the flower analogy," Abby quipped, beginning to enjoy the sparring.

He shot her a quick, assessing glance before returning his attention to his driving. "Are you deliberately baiting me, Abby?"

"Perhaps. Does it annoy you?"

"No. I consider it a good sign. If you're trying to provoke me, you must not be terribly afraid of me."

The serious remark was irritating, Abby discovered. "I'm not sure I like being analyzed."

"There are a lot of things you don't like, aren't there?" he observed casually as he pulled into another tiny curb-side parking space. The man had a talent for parking cars in nonexistent spaces, Abby had to admit to herself.

"A woman is entitled to a few opinions," she declared regally.

"And a man is entitled to try to change her mind on occasion," he responded with a grim little smile that barely shaped his mouth.

"Are you often successful?" she challenged as she allowed him to guide her into the plush, dimly lit restaurant.

"I rarely make the effort to change a woman's mind."

"Should I be flattered?"

"It's not a question of flattery," he explained precisely.

"I had a feeling it wouldn't be." Laughter lit her eyes as she glanced up at him. "More of a business decision perhaps?"

He stared down at her for a moment before answering. "I told you in the car that once I have come to a decision—slow and ponderous though the process may be—I do whatever is required to bring about a successful conclusion to the project. I've made my basic decision concerning you."

"Is that a warning?" Some of the amusement died in her eyes.

"No, Abby, it's a statement of fact. Take my advice and don't let it ruin your evening, though. We have hours and hours ahead of us. I'd hate to have you sulking through to the bitter end."

"I never sulk," she assured him tranquilly. Then she turned and smiled brilliantly at the approaching maître d', effectively cutting off the conversation.

They were led to an intimate booth, the table in front of them laid with gleaming silver and snowy linen. A low-voiced discussion between Torr and the wine steward went on for several minutes, and Abby used the opportunity to rummage about in her small evening bag for a couple of tablets.

Torr glanced at her just as she was popping them into her mouth. "More stress vitamins?"

"Calcium. Good for bones and teeth."

"Have you tried drinking more milk instead?" he asked laconically.

"I hate milk." She downed the tablets with several sips from the water goblet. Then she grinned. "I much prefer wine. What are we having tonight?"

"There's a new sauvignon blanc I've been curious about that's in from one of my favorite California wineries. I thought it would go nicely with the smoked salmon and capers."

"What smoked salmon and capers?"

"The smoked salmon and capers we're having as an appetizer," he spelled out calmly.

"I don't recall ordering an appetizer. I haven't even glanced at the menu!" Irritation at his presumption made her glare at him severely.

"Anyone who eats calcium tablets as an appetizer doesn't deserve to get a look at the menu. How many pills do you take a day?"

"I haven't counted," she told him frostily.

"Are you your own best customer?"

"Believe me, the various people who sell vitamins and minerals door-to-door for me have a lot of customers who take far more pills than I do!"

"And you can really make a living off of this, hmmm?" He eyed her reflectively. "Is that your only source of income?"

She sent him a speculative glance. "What's the matter? Do you normally only date rich women? Afraid I won't be able to keep you in the style to which you would like to become accustomed?"

"You are getting feisty, aren't you? A few more cracks like that and I might leave you with the tab for tonight's dinner," he advised her blandly.

"More threats?" she asked interestedly as the wine arrived.

"Abby, honey, I've already explained I don't issue threats or warnings. I merely make statements of fact." He accepted the sample of wine, taking a moment to savor it carefully. Then he nodded firmly. "I asked about your vitamin business because I was wondering if it's full time for you."

"My only source of income," she assured him cheerfully as the waiter finished pouring the wine and discreetly left. "Unless you want to count the shares of stock I inherited from my uncle."

"Shares in what company?" Torr lounged back comfortably and sipped his wine with appreciation.

"The one my uncle founded. Lyndon Technologies is based in Seattle. It's a privately held firm that has something to do with computers," Abby explained carelessly. "My cousin holds the largest portion of the shares. The rest are scattered around the family. I own about twenty percent, one of the bigger chunks. The only reason I got any at all was because my father loaned my uncle the money to get started. My father told him to pay off the loan in shares of stock held in trust for me. I received them a few years ago when Uncle Bert died. The company has done nothing but lose money for the past five years, though, so the stock isn't worth anything. The hope is that my cousin's husband—he's the president—will be able to salvage things." Abby reached for her wine and took a fair-size swallow. She didn't want to discuss the subject any further. Thoughts of her cousin Cynthia brought thoughts of Cynthia's husband, Ward Tyson, to mind. And those thoughts led uneasily to the brochure for the Misty Inn resort.

"Your cousin's husband is a good businessman?"

"Supposedly he is," she said with dismissal in her voice as she picked up the menu. "Let's see. Since you've committed us to the smoked salmon, I think I might have something along the lines of the veal with morels. And perhaps a nice romaine lettuce salad," she went on industriously, studying the list of elegant food.

"You can forget the veal and salad," Torr said simply, plucking the menu out of her hands. "We're having squid."

"Squid!" She stared at him.

"In an herbed wine sauce," he continued. "You'll love it."

"How do you know?" she demanded through clenched teeth.

"Because squid is loaded with vitamins and minerals." He pulled the wine bottle out of the ice bucket and poured some more of the sauvignon blanc into her glass.

Abby leveled a long, considering stare at him as he went through the action of pouring the wine. She found herself aware of something besides the basic, solid strength in him; she also recognized an intrinsic, masculine grace. And that made her remember the elegantly restrained flower designs he had created in class. Her copper-red nails beat a tiny tattoo on the white tablecloth and her contemplative expression became a frown.

"Anything wrong?" Torr asked politely.

"Do you mind telling me why?" she demanded coolly.

"Of course not, but you'll have to clarify the question. Why what?"

"Why, for a man who can create an impression of an entire spring garden with just a few leaves and a daffodil or two, you are being so heavy-handed tonight?"

"Ah, the squid." He nodded complacently.

"Actually, I meant the arrogance, not the squid in particular," she said sweetly. "You seem to forget that

I've seen just how subtle you can be in class. I know you're quite capable of elegance and finesse and that means you're probably quite capable of politeness on a date. So why are you playing the overbearing, domineering male who won't even allow his companion to select her own meal?"

He thought about that for a moment, as if deciding how to explain himself. A tiny smile edged the line of his mouth and the amber eyes were unreadable. But he didn't pretend to misunderstand.

"Because a bit of arrogance with regard to something as mundane as the food provides you with a convenient target. A focal point, I suppose," he finally said. "It gives you something to complain about and criticize and rail against without giving you something to really worry over. Doing things like choosing food for you without consultation is annoying, but it doesn't frighten you. And it absorbs your attention so you don't have time to worry about what's going to happen when I take you home later."

Abby sat very still, taking in the full implications of his words. "My God," she breathed eventually and not without genuine admiration, "a red herring."

"Squid," he corrected indulgently, eyes gleaming.

She shook her head. "That was very clever of you."

"Not so clever. You realized right away I was up to something," he replied sighing, and sitting back as the salmon and capers arrived.

"No, no," she denied firmly, "I'm impressed. I mean, naturally, I was aware you could be exercising a good deal more in the way of social grace if you wanted to do so, but I don't think I would ever have guessed exactly why you were playing the arrogant lord and master. I would simply have continued to stay mildly annoyed all evening. And I wouldn't have had time to worry about later."

"But now that you're on to me, you're going to start worrying?" He slid a paper-thin slice of smoked salmon onto a toast point and added a caper or two. Then he gravely held it out to her, his gaze intent.

"Should I?" Abby hesitated and then accepted the salmon offering.

"Worry about later? No. You won't have to fight me off at the end of the evening." The words were spoken with sure, steady promise.

Abby paused a moment longer, holding the toast point at her lips. She believed him, she realized. She wasn't quite certain why she should, but she did. Making her decision in her usual impulsive manner she parted her lips and sank her neat, white teeth firmly into the toast and salmon. "Okay, Torr. I won't worry about later."

"Just like that?"

She lifted one shoulder delicately. "I'm not nearly as subtle as you, and I usually make my decisions fairly quickly."

"And you've decided to trust me?" he pressed.

"Yes." She gave him a rueful glance, full of laughter. "Must be the result of watching you in class for the past few weeks. You were always so careful and gentle with the flowers," she explained wistfully. And the end result had always been that the flowers had done exactly as he wished, she reminded herself with a dash of warning. Her designs had always gone wildly out of control, but Torr's had behaved precisely as he had wanted them to behave.

"Thank you, Abby."

"Now about that squid," she began.

"I told you. You're going to love it."

"But, Torr!" The humor in her was threatening to spoil the royal protest, however, and she knew he'd seen it.

"Abby, honey, I keep telling you that I'm not nearly as subtle as you seem to think. I really do think you're going to like the squid and I intend that you should try it."

"Why do I have the strangest feeling you've never been married?" she countered, surrendering to the inevitable with good grace. To her astonishment the throwaway remark seemed to catch him off guard. He looked up quickly from the slice of salmon he was about to center on a toast point and there wasn't a trace of amusement in the amber depths of his eyes.

"I was married," he told her evenly.

Instantly Abby realized she'd overstepped some invisible boundary. "I'm sorry, Torr. I didn't mean to dredge up any bad memories. It was only a little joke. I just meant to imply that because of your casual arrogance I assumed no woman had had an opportunity to, er, whip you into shape...." Her voice trailed off uneasily as she racked her brain for another topic of conversation.

"It's all right," he finally said quietly. "I was married for two years. My wife ... drowned in a swimming accident three years ago. I don't generally discuss it."

"No, no, I certainly understand," Abby said hurriedly. "There are things I don't care to talk about either. Please forgive me?" Impulsively she put out her long-nailed fingers and touched the dark sleeve of his jacket where his arm lay casually on the table.

Torr looked down at her fingers and then he folded his own square hand over hers. Abby felt as if he'd enveloped it but it wasn't an unpleasant sensation, rather a warm and comforting feeling. Almost a gesture of protection, she decided, breaking into a smile.

He returned the smile and in the silent moment of communication that took place between them, Abby knew the tone of the evening had been set. She relaxed even further and knew that she was genuinely going to enjoy her time with Torr Latimer.

Something flickered in Torr's eyes as he watched her face, an emotion that might have been either relief or satisfaction. Abby decided not to worry about it. She told herself she wouldn't worry about anything else that evening, in fact.

The conversation went easily from one topic to another, bringing lighthearted arguments, unexpected agreements and a pleasurable contentment. The squid was delicious, just as Torr had predicted, and Abby was feeling sufficiently magnanimous to tell him so.

"I'm glad you enjoyed it," he said as he escorted her back out to the car and assisted her inside.

"What?" she challenged laughingly. "You're not going to say 'I told you so'?"

"I wouldn't dream of it. I know when I'm ahead," he added with a hint of amusement. "And now I'm going to take you home, kiss you good-night at your door and hope you'll say yes when I ask you out for tomorrow."

Abby held her breath. "Where would you like to take me tomorrow?" she whispered.

"The rose gardens," he answered unhesitatingly as he pulled away from the curb.

"That sounds wonderful. I'd love to go." The decision had been made somewhere during dinner. She wanted to see Torr Latimer again. Portland's rose gardens were a source of city pride, and although she had been to them on several occasions, the promised visit with Torr was going to be very special. She sank back into the leather seat of the BMW and contemplated the night and the man beside her. Both seemed exciting, and both contained an element of the unknown, and she realized she felt a sense of anticipation about both which she hadn't experienced in a long, long time.

"Are you really going to kiss me good-night at my door?" She dared to tease lightly, goaded by an inner need to explore the anticipation and excitement that had been building in her all evening.

He threw her a hooded, speculative glance before answering. "Unless you invite me inside, yes. Worried?"

"No." Then she realized just how true that was. "I don't feel worried about anything at all tonight," she added with a sense of wonder.

"Good. When I watched you breaking daffodils and running wild with that flower arrangement last night, wilder than usual, that is, I wondered if something might be bothering you."

Only that brochure showing up unexpectedly in her mail, she answered silently. But she had rationalized that to her own satisfaction. It was purely a fluke. She had simply gotten on the resort's advertising list.

"Right now the world seems quite perfect," she assured him easily.

"It rarely stays that way for long."

"Spoilsport."

He found another nearly hidden space on the street outside her apartment house, switched off the ignition and turned to face her in the intimate darkness. "I'm serious, Abby."

"You're always serious."

"I meant what I said. The world rarely stays perfect for very long," he continued huskily.

"Are you about to give me a lecture on how we must live for today because tomorrow could bring disaster?" she mocked. "Is this a prelude to trying to seduce me with that old line about living for the moment and taking our pleasures while we can?" The first hint of frost was coating her words now as she realized the lovely evening was about to end.

His dark head moved in a clear rejection of the accusation. "No, I'm only saying that if something is wrong, if your world is less than perfect when you wake up in the morning, I'll be around to deal with it."

Startled by the intensity in his words, Abby lifted her copper nails to touch the side of his face. "That's very kind of you, Torr," she murmured unsteadily.

He caught her fingers and crushed them with a degree of force that was one step beyond gentle. "I've told you before not to expect kindness from me and there's a catch to the deal I'm offering."

The softness in Abby's face froze into a distant, aloof expression. She tried to free her hand and found it trapped where he pinned it to his shoulder. "There usually is a catch to the most interesting 'deals,'" she said sarcastically.

"I'm glad you're businesswoman enough to understand that."

"What are you about to imply now, Torr? That I'm going to have to sleep with you in order to continue to enjoy the pleasure of your company?"

Again he shook his head in a slow, sure negative. "The only string I'm putting on this relationship, Abby, is that I want to be sure I'm the only man in your world. If there's someone else who thinks he has a claim on you, I want you to tell him goodbye. And I want you to get rid of him before you sleep with me."

Abby wrenched herself free, flung open the car door and leapt lightly out onto the sidewalk. "You certainly do know how to ruin a lovely evening!"

He was beside her before she found the key to the lobby door and she knew she wouldn't get rid of him until he had seen her upstairs to her apartment. They rode the elevator in silence. Her chin lifted forbiddingly as she swept down the hall.

"Abby—"

"Listen to me, Torr," she gritted. "I've been taking care of matters, perfect and otherwise, in my world for quite some time. I don't need anyone to look after me and I'm not about to make any 'deals' to get protection I don't require. Furthermore, just for your information, I would never give any man who demanded them exclusive rights over me. Men who feel they have to ask for them rarely believe a woman who makes such promises, anyway. Men like that are incapable of trust. They are possessive and quite willing to make life unbearable for a woman."

"If you've finished with the lecture, Abby," Torr began grimly as she found her apartment key, "I'd like a chance to talk this problem over in a civilized fashion."

"There won't be time. You're going to say good-night here at my door, remember?"

He reached out to catch her wrist as she turned the key in the lock and pushed open the door. When she would have stepped inside to safety he pulled her up short.

Quite unexpectedly Abby's right foot slipped out from under her. The delicate high heel had skidded awkwardly on a scrap of paper lying on the hardwood floor and the additional impetus of Torr's forceful grasp combined to send her tumbling heavily against him.

"Oh!" Her surprise was muffled against the fabric of his jacket as she instinctively clutched for support. Automatically Torr's arms closed around Abby, steadying her but not releasing her.

"What the . . . ?" He glanced down at her feet in frowning concern.

"You have no business manhandling me like this!" Rigidly Abby found her balance and tried to push herself away from him.

"I didn't cause you to lose your balance. You must have slipped on that envelope."

"What envelope?" She pushed aside a pale tendril of hair that had escaped the loosely arranged topknot and fallen into her eyes. Then she stared at Torr as he released her to lean down and pick up the white object on the floor. Wordlessly he straightened and handed it to her.

"I must have dropped it earlier," she mumbled, brows attempting to knit across the top of her nose.

"It's addressed to you and it looks as if it was slipped under your door," Torr pointed out.

He was right, of course. She didn't recognize the envelope and had certainly not dropped one addressed to herself earlier before leaving the apartment. Her name and address were neatly typed on the outside. Quickly Abby tore it open, wondering which of her neighbors had left a message for her.

"It's probably from Mrs. Wilkins down the hall wanting me to water her plants while she goes off to see her new grandson." Abby lifted out the stiff piece of paper that was inside the envelope. As she saw what she held, she nearly dropped it.

Stunned to a level of momentary numbness, Abby stared at the color photograph in her hand. No, it couldn't be! It wasn't possible. Her mind felt curiously blank.

"What is it, Abby?" Torr moved to glance over her shoulder.

His interest in the photograph broke the short, shattering spell that had gripped her. "Just a photo I loaned Mrs. Wilkins the other day. She wanted to see some pictures of my last vacation." In another second or two, Abby knew, she would be descending into outright babble. She had to get rid of Torr immediately. She needed time to think, time to assimilate the full implications of the shocking photograph. Hastily she shoved the picture back into the envelope and whirled to face him.

He was studying her with the cool, assessing gaze that she had grown accustomed to during their classes in flower arranging. There were times when she had found the intensity of that gaze almost amusing. Tonight it was terrifying.

"Good night, Torr. Thank you for a very *interesting* evening."

He watched her a moment longer and she nearly panicked as she realized she couldn't predict exactly what he would do next. She wanted him out of the apartment at all costs, but what on earth could she do if he opted to stay?

"I'll pick you up around one o'clock tomorrow," he finally said.

"Yes, yes, one will be fine. I'll be ready," she answered him far too quickly.

When he reached for her she shrank back nervously, a protest on her lips.

"My good-night kiss, remember?" he prompted very softly.

She didn't argue. It seemed the fastest way to get rid of him. Obediently Abby turned her face up for his kiss, her fingers hovering against his shoulders. If he was surprised by her meek behavior, Torr did not comment on it. Instead he folded her close until she felt overwhelmed by the heat and strength of him and then he fastened his mouth on hers.

For a traumatic moment Abby was almost over-powered by a dangerous longing to simply surrender to the virile strength that surrounded her. The temptation was wholly unexpected and beyond anything she could have imagined. His kiss fused her to him, promising passion and protection, and she moaned softly far back in her throat as she realized the danger and the desire that threatened to take control.

He held her deeply in thrall for several long seconds and then, reluctantly, Torr released her. The knowledge that she had been on the edge of belonging to him, even if only for the space of one kiss, flared through his awareness, arousing him and urging him to pull her back into his arms.

But there was too much uncertainty in the air, too many unexplained factors between them yet. He was not a boy, Torr told himself grimly. He could wait. Rushing things now might well ruin everything.

"Good night, Abby. I'll see you tomorrow. I found our evening together *interesting*, too." With a wry smile he let himself quietly out the door and heard the lock being slipped into place behind him.

The memory of her silvered blue eyes stayed with him as he climbed into the BMW and started home. Abby had wonderfully expressive eyes, he reflected coolly. At various times during the evening he had seen laughter and warmth and even excitement mirrored in the silvery pools.

But when he'd shut the door of her apartment behind himself the expression in her eyes hadn't been anything close to laughter or warmth or excitement. Instead, her gaze had been filled with a new and unfathomable tension. She was probably even now taking one of her vitamin tonics for the problem.

Torr's face settled into its customary hard lines as he drove through the city streets. What had that business with the photograph been about, he asked himself. It had been a picture of Abby and someone else—a man, he felt certain, although the second figure hadn't been as focused. And the setting had been the parking lot of a large motel.

Motel? Or a resort? The resort that had been pictured in the brochure lying on her kitchen counter the night before?

What game was Abby playing and how long would he give her before yanking her out of the action?

The question kept him awake long into the night.

3

THE PHONE RANG IN Abby's kitchen at nine the next morning. She glanced at the clock with a sense of shock as she roused herself from bed, found a robe and went to answer the imperious summons. Nine o'clock! She never slept that late. But the previous night had been a restless one and when sleep had eventually come, it had been filled with nightmares of winter on the coast and even more disturbing dreams of a man with black hair and amber eyes—a man who offered passion even as he offered an undefined sense of menace.

"Cynthia!" The sound of her cousin's voice calling from Seattle only added to Abby's growing tension.

"Oh, sorry, Abby, did I wake you? You're always such an early riser," Cynthia apologized cheerfully. "And now that I've got Laura I've discovered the joys of early rising myself."

"Most new mothers complain about the upset in their schedules after the babies arrive," Abby managed to say with a reasonable note of lightheartedness in her voice. Cynthia was almost the last person she wanted to talk to this morning. Stifling a groan, she perched on a stool and propped her elbow on the counter. "How's baby Laura doing?"

"Great! Hungry as a little piglet at the moment. I'm feeding her while I chat with you. How's the vitamin business?"

"Thanks for reminding me," Abby said with genuine gratitude as she reached for a nearby bottle. "I haven't taken my iron yet today." She unscrewed the cap and gulped a couple of the black tablets. Then she leaned over the counter and ran water into a glass.

"You and your pills," Cynthia said, sighing.

"I need the energy."

"No kidding! Late night?"

"Don't sound so enthusiastic about it," Abby complained, reaching for another bottle. It wouldn't hurt to take a few more B vitamins. Her nerves weren't feeling so great this morning.

"But I am enthusiastic. You've been living like a nun for so long—"

"Cynthia, that's not true and you know it." Abby decided to take two of the vitamin B tablets on the theory that if one was good, two were better.

"It is true. You haven't had a serious relationship since you were involved with that real-estate executive two years ago."

"I date. I'm not living like a recluse." Abby protested more as a matter of form than because she thought it would influence Cynthia. Her cousin had spent the past couple of years growing increasingly concerned about Abby's policy of arm's-length relationships.

"Dating and having a wild affair are two different things, Abby. It's time you had an affair."

"Gee, thanks. Got anyone in mind for me?"

"That," Cynthia announced grandly, "is precisely why I'm calling today. I am going to introduce you to a very interesting vice president whom Ward just hired. You're going to love him. About thirty-five, divorced, good-looking..."

"Oh, Cynthia. Not another one." Abby bit her lip, her gaze falling on the damning photograph on the counter near the vitamin C tablets.

"I'm thinking of a small dinner party on the eighteenth. How about it? We'll keep it casual, of course. Ward won't have any trouble getting John to come. After all, Ward's his boss. I think I'll fix poached salmon and—"

"Cynthia, please."

"Was the guy who kept you up last night any more interesting than the one I'm offering?" her cousin challenged spiritedly. "How did you meet him?"

Abby was staring so hard at the out-of-focus image of the man in the photograph that she almost misunderstood the question. Then she realized Cynthia was referring to Torr and not the man in the photo. "In a class I've been taking on the art of Japanese flower arrangement," she told her.

"A class on flower arrangement! Good grief! Abby, he's probably gay or something. What kind of man takes classes in flower arrangement?"

"An unusual one," Abby admitted dryly. "And I'm pretty sure he's not gay."

"Hmmmm." Cynthia broke off thoughtfully and Abby could almost see the wheels turning inside her cousin's beautiful head. "Were you, uh, testing to make sure last night? Is he still there?"

"No, he's not here," Abby heard herself retort irritably. "Cynthia, stop worrying about me. I'm doing fine, really I am."

"Abby, after you spent so much time worrying about me this past winter, you must know it's only natural for me to be concerned about you now."

"People always worry about mothers-to-be," Abby tried to say lightly.

"Especially mothers-to-be whose marriages have suddenly taken a nosedive, right? It was a little rocky there for a while, wasn't it?" Cynthia's voice held remembered pain and fear.

Abby heard a crinkling sound and looked down to find she had begun to crumple the photograph. Angrily she finished the job. "Cynthia? Everything's okay now, isn't it?"

"Oh, Abby, I've never been happier," her cousin assured her, sounding very certain. "It was just that everything happened at once shortly before the baby was born. Ward had all those problems at work and he was under a great deal of strain. And I was solely concerned with the baby. Then, after Laura was born I had my hands full and there just wasn't time enough to be both mother and wife. Thank heavens I realized I had to get hold of myself and the situation before everything went to pieces. Life is just perfect now. Maybe we owe it all to those vitamin tonics you insisted I take."

"Can I get your name on a letter of endorsement?" Abby tried to project a smile through the teasing words.

"Always the businesswoman! But I'm serious. Maybe all those pills you fed me did some good. All I know for certain is that I would have been a basket case if Ward had walked out on me. He's the most important person in my world. Even Laura will have to take second place to my husband, I'm afraid."

Abby heard the feminine intent and decision in her cousin's words and swallowed awkwardly. Ward was the most important person in Cynthia's life. Her cousin would be crushed if she were standing beside Abby and looking down at the crumpled photograph on the counter. Tears stung Abby's eyes. Tears of rage and a nameless fear.

"Abby. Are you still there?"

"I'm here."

"Oh, I thought we'd been cut off for a moment. I've got to hang up. Laura needs changing and the little devil has just spit up all over me."

"The joys of motherhood," Abby murmured.

"Go ahead and laugh. I've never been happier. I've got it all, Abby. How many women are this lucky?"

"Not many."

"Going to see the man from last night again?"

"This afternoon."

"Good. Where are you going?" Cynthia demanded.

"To the rose gardens."

"The rose gardens! Abby, are you quite sure he's, well, a viable candidate?"

"Believe me, I'm sure! Goodbye, Cynthia. Thanks for calling."

"Have fun! And keep the eighteenth free just in case."

Fun, thought Abby as she hung up the phone, was about the last thing on her mind. She climbed down off the stool and started toward the bathroom for her morning shower. It was then that she spotted the second envelope on the floor just inside the front door.

Even before she bent to retrieve it with trembling fingers, Abby was certain it would contain another photograph. With a sense of dread she clumsily unsealed the envelope and slowly pulled out the color print inside.

In this shot there was no mistaking the identity of the man. His profile had been clearly caught and held as he walked out of the hotel room beside a woman. This time the scrap of ocean in the background made it plain that the location was a coastal one. Abby wanted to cry out with anger and frustration as she studied the other image in the photograph. The woman beside the man was herself.

For a long moment she simply stood staring at the print, her mind reeling with the implications. Someone had taken photos of her during that weekend she had spent at the beach this past winter. Someone had followed her and taken pictures of herself and a man clearly sharing a weekend together. Someone had stood right outside her front door, literally stalked her. Abby shuddered. Why?

Over and over the question pounded through her brain. Why would someone do such a thing? In a gesture of restless anxiety she turned the print around between her fingers. She was concentrating on it so furiously that it was several seconds before Abby realized there was another slip of paper inside the envelope.

The note, she thought distractedly. This must be the note. Wasn't there always a note with blackmail threats? Oh, God. She was becoming hysterical. She yanked out the slip of paper and quickly read the type-written message.

There are other pictures. Several of them. The kind of pictures that could ruin a marriage such as your cousin's. But all things are negotiable, aren't they?

It was unsigned, naturally. Abby's teeth clenched together as she realized the extent of her helplessness. Fury battled with fear, sending her nerves into a fragile state. Her pulse raced with adrenaline but there was no outlet for either of her instinctive responses—fight or flight.

Her mind began to whirl in useless, agitated circles, making it virtually impossible to think straight. Desperately she tried to collect her thoughts, pacing the living room with frantic strides. There was no way to fight the shadowy blackmailer. She had no idea who it was or when he would appear in person. Abby felt like a sitting duck waiting for the bullet from the hunter's gun.

Her steps became more restless. Twice she struck a stray box of vitamins with her foot. When she almost tripped over the box a third time, Abby kicked at the green-and-gold package with frustrated panic. She had to do something more constructive than pace her living room. This was going to get her precisely nowhere. Wondering wildly what other people did when confronted with situations like this, she tried to force herself to outline her options.

The short list that occurred to her was hardly inspiring. In fact, its meagerness generated increasing panic.

Her world narrowed down to the threat represented by the photos and the instinctive need to protect Cynthia. Nothing else mattered. She was a cornered creature who had to take some decisive action or find herself being maneuvered by an unknown hunter. Abby froze at that thought. She would not sit here and wait for her fate! There had to be something she could do to protect herself and Cynthia.

Chewing unconsciously on her lip, she forced herself to go to the window and gaze unseeingly out at the morning Oregon mist. She would not remain here and cower. Priorities must be set. She had to find out who was behind all this. She had to *do* something! But there was nothing, no one tangible yet, to fight.

Which left only the flight response, Abby decided abruptly. Whirling, she headed for the bedroom. The blackmailer couldn't do much if he or she couldn't reach the victim. There was always the possibility that he might go straight to Cynthia with the pictures, but that didn't seem entirely logical. There was no money to be had that way.

No, it seemed more probable that the blackmailer would first try to find the intended victim. And if the intended victim were out of town, it might just give Abby the breathing space she needed to figure out what was going on and who was attempting to threaten her.

The decision to run gave her a sense of taking some action instead of offering herself as an easy target. It was an illusory sense of action. She knew it even as she showered, dressed in jeans and a narrow ribbed-knit red sweater, and began to pack. But instinct told her that the blackmailer would seek her out and if it took a while to hunt her down, she might be able to use that time to do something constructive. If she could lure whoever it was out into the open, identify him or her, she might be able to retaliate.

Not knowing how long she would be gone, Abby forced herself to pack carefully. It was April, early spring in the Pacific Northwest and that meant the weather was still chilly most days. She piled sweaters and slacks into her largest suitcase and then selected enough underwear to last for a week. She could always wash out necessities in a hotel room.

Hotel room. What hotel room? Where was she going to go, she asked herself. And what about the deliveries scheduled to be picked up during the week by her salespeople?

More time was spent as she got on the phone and arranged to have her top saleswoman handle distribution. Gail Farley was willing, if mildly surprised.

"Sure, I'll come over right now and collect the boxes. But when will you be back, Abby?"

"I'm not sure. Something's come up and I could be gone a couple of weeks. I'll tell the apartment manager to let you into my place if you need more supplies, okay?"

Then there was the impatient wait for Gail to arrive and collect enough boxes to last the salespeople for at least a week. By the time the other woman had driven off with a selection of MegaLife products stacked high in the back seat of her car, it was after twelve.

Abby took a last glance around the apartment and then spotted her own private collection of vitamin bottles. Hastily she gathered them up and dumped them into a small zippered bag. If she'd ever needed vitamins and minerals, it was now! Just before she closed the bag she reached inside, retrieved the bottle of vitamin C tablets and popped a couple into her mouth. This was no time to leave herself open to the possibility of colds or flu.

Abby wondered if she might have overpacked when she realized she could hardly drag her large suitcase to the front door. But how could anyone guess how long she'd be gone in a situation like this? Better to have overpacked than underpacked. With a great deal of pushing and shoving she got the case into position by the door and was going back to the bedroom for her coat when the doorbell rang.

It was then that she remembered the date with Torr Latimer. A horrified glance at the clock showed that it was ten to one.

"Damn!" Now she was going to have to make up some very hasty explanations for breaking the date. Why hadn't she thought to telephone him earlier? He probably wasn't going to appreciate arriving at her door and discovering that she was on her way out of town.

"I'm awfully sorry. I was just going to call you," she began firmly as she threw open the door and found him standing there. He was dressed in his usual conservative style, wearing a tan long-sleeved shirt and dark brown slacks. A soft suede jacket was folded neatly over one arm. Abby realized it must be drizzling rain outside because there was a glistening dampness about his dark hair.

Torr looked down at her without saying a word for a moment, taking in the slightly frazzled look of her carelessly combed hair and the well-worn jeans.

"Call me about what?" he finally asked reasonably.

"I'm afraid I'm going to have to go out of town," she said quickly, struggling for a viable explanation. "Very unexpected. Just got a call from relatives. You'll have to excuse me, I'm feeling a little hassled. Been packing all morning and I . . ."

"Where are you going?" he demanded gently, stepping forward with such implacable intent that she automatically gave ground.

"The, uh, the coast," she answered, thinking that sounded as reasonable as anywhere else. "I'm going to spend a week or two on the coast."

His amber eyes narrowed. "At the resort where you spent a weekend during the winter?"

Abby paled at the reference to the scene of her present disaster. Torr couldn't know, of course. He was just taking a guess based on having seen that brochure lying on the counter. Deliberately she cleared her throat. "Actually, I'll be staying a bit north of there this time. My relatives have a place near Lincoln City."

"How long will you be gone?" He moved away from her as he spoke, stalking across the vanilla carpet with a seemingly directionless grace.

"Oh, a week or so," Abby tried to say lightly. She frowned anxiously as he wandered toward the kitchen counter. The crumpled photograph she had received the night before still lay where she had left it while talking to Cynthia. He didn't appear to notice it, however.

"A little sudden, isn't it?" He lounged negligently on a stool, one foot braced against the floor, the other hooked over a rung.

A cold chill coursed down Abby's spine. She didn't like the laconic attitude and she didn't care for the casual questions he was throwing at her. It was time to take a firmer hand. "I just got the call this morning. My aunt wants to spend some time by the sea and she needs someone to look after her. It's a great opportunity for me to take a few days off and enjoy the ocean." Abby made a show of glancing at her watch. "I really should be on my way. It's getting late and I promised I'd be there by dinner. She's the type who will worry, poor dear."

"I'm the type who worries, too." A strange ghost of a smile touched his mouth.

Abby stared at him, uncertain of his mood. "What about?" she asked flatly.

"Oh, this and that."

"Torr..."

"I might worry, for example, about why you would break a date with no notice just to rush off to visit auntie. Or I might worry about why you look so tense and flustered when all you've got planned is a drive to the coast to stay with a relative." His large hand shifted suddenly on the counter, closing over the crumpled photograph. "Then again," he went on musingly, "I might worry about the real reason you've suddenly decided to take off for the coast. It seems to be a popular vacation retreat for you."

"I happen to like the coast," she muttered, experiencing a twinge of genuine panic. Dealing with Torr was taking on overtones of dealing with an unpredictable beast. It wasn't fair! She had enough on her mind.

"So do I. Maybe auntie would like to have an extra houseguest. Why don't you invite me along, Abby?"

Her mouth fell open in shock. "Invite you along?" she squeaked. "Torr, that's impossible! My aunt's place is very small and she doesn't like strangers. Besides, I can't just . . . just invite you to spend a week or so with me! For heaven's sake, I hardly know you."

"I'll stay at a nearby motel if you feel your aunt wouldn't want an extra person in the house."

"Torr, you're being ridiculous!"

"No more ridiculous than you're being trying to convince me you've got a sudden invitation from an aunt that you have to honor." He paused and frowned at her. "You weren't even going to call me, were you? You were on your way out the door when I arrived. What's the matter, Abby? Do you always jump this fast when he calls? I would have thought you'd have more pride."

"When who calls?" she whispered blankly.

Torr carefully flattened the crumpled photograph and glanced down at the male figure in the picture. "Him. The guy you go to the coast with so often."

Abby swallowed nervously, her eyes never leaving Torr's hard face. "You know nothing about this. And I'm under no obligation to explain myself to you. It's time you left, Torr."

"I'm not leaving without the truth," he stated quietly.

"And if you don't happen to like the truth or believe it?" she retorted.

"Then I probably won't leave at all. At least, not without taking you with me."

Her mouth went dry. "Torr, you can't do this."

"Do what? All I'm asking for is an explanation."

"I've given you one! As well as an apology for breaking our date. What more do you think you're entitled to, anyway? Torr, I don't owe you anything!"

"Are you in love with him?"

"In love with who?" she yelped furiously.

"The man in the photograph."

"No, I am not in love with him!"

"Then why are you dashing off to spend a week on the coast with the man?"

"I am not going to spend the week with Ward!" Abby shut her eyes in self-disgust as she realized how much she'd been goaded into saying.

"Ward?"

"Never mind. Just leave, Torr. Please. I have to get out of here."

"I'd like a last name to pin on him," Torr remarked placidly, studying the photo.

"Well, you can wait until hell freezes over!"

He glanced up, his gaze still and strangely frightening. "Don't you know," Torr uttered very softly, "that the outer reaches of hell are already frozen? Hell is a very cold place, Abby. Not a warm one. Cold and infinitely lonely."

In that moment Abby recognized with great certainty that Torr Latimer knew what he was talking about. They regarded each other across the distance of the room. Abby was aware that she wasn't going to get rid of this man without giving him some answers.

"Believe what you want to believe," she finally said wearily. "It doesn't really matter, anyway."

"Try telling me the truth. I think I'll believe it when I hear it."

She moved restlessly, going across the room to sink down onto the sofa. "I don't want to talk about it, Torr. Please. Go away."

He stood up with a smooth, lithe movement that made her flinch. He crossed the room before she could get to her feet and an instant later his strong hands closed around her upper arms. He lifted her off the couch until she stood facing him, her face stark with helpless defiance.

"Is the man in the photograph your lover?" Each word was delivered with the impact of a body blow.

Fear came to Abby then. The kind of fear she had dreaded experiencing again with a man. With it came a fierce determination not to be crushed by it.

"I've told you he's not my lover."

"Who is he?"

"I don't wish to tell you that."

"Abby, you're going to tell me."

"And if I don't?" The challenge took all of her courage. She could feel his blunt fingers sinking deeply into the flesh of her arms and the strength of him made her catch her breath.

"You will." It wasn't a threat. As Torr had explained, he simply made statements of fact. Quite suddenly Abby believed him.

"My cousin's husband," she whispered. "Ward Tyson. The man who runs Lyndon Technologies, my uncle's computer firm."

"And you're not on your way to spend the week with him?"

"No!"

"But you spent a weekend with him this past winter?"

"That's none of your business!" she hissed.

He said nothing but his big hands moved up her arms to curl around her throat. The fear smashed through her in a sudden burst and she opened her mouth to scream.

He stifled the cry with his lips, crushed them beneath his own with an intensity that robbed her of breath. Frozen with panic, she went utterly still, waiting for the tightening of his fingers around her throat. Her eyes stayed open and her body was taut under his touch. She would fight, she vowed silently.

But the big, blunt fingers on her throat never tightened. And while his mouth took control and coolly dominated hers, the kiss was not one of violence. For a timeless moment Abby braced herself for cruelty. It wasn't until she felt his fingers gently massaging the nape of her neck, attempting to draw a response from her, that she understood Torr was not going to hurt her. The relief was as enervating as the fear had been paralyzing.

"Abby," he groaned huskily. "Abby, why are you so afraid of me?"

She recalled the way he handled flowers, and sagged against him, taking in air in huge gulps as he allowed her to lay her head on his shoulder. His palms moved along her spine now, soothing and assuring. Abby began to realize that there could be comfort in a man's strength. The thought was enough to make her head spin.

"Torr, none of this affects you," she got out in a painful voice. "Please believe me. I have to go."

"Then I'll go with you," he muttered into her hair. "And I'll keep you with me until you tell me the whole story. Don't you think I know something is very, very wrong? You've been nervous since the last night of class. And when that photograph arrived, don't you think I saw the way it affected you? Abby, what happened this morning? Why were you going to pack and leave without even remembering to cancel our date?"

"I can't explain. I'm not even sure myself what's going on. I don't want you involved, Torr," she whispered honestly.

"I am involved. Honey, I'm going to keep you with me night and day until I find out exactly what's going on."

"You can't!"

"Do you really believe you can stop me? Abby, very soon I'm going to be your lover. I have a right to protect you."

She shook her head, feeling trapped by his strength and his intent perseverance. She had a premonition that it might ultimately be impossible to deny this man anything. "You can't say that. You don't know what will happen between us. Torr, be reasonable. Can't you accept my word that you shouldn't get involved?"

"No. And I'm being perfectly reasonable because I do know what will happen between us. I've known since the night I took you home after class."

"Torr, I won't let you take control of me like this!" The protest was faint but it carried determination. "I won't be rushed into a relationship I'm not sure I want and I won't let you assume rights I'm not prepared to give."

"Then we'll just sit here in your living room and talk about it until you are willing to be rushed into a relationship with me and until you are willing to give me some rights."

She could hear the lazy amusement in his voice and her head jerked up as annoyance began to replace some of the hopelessness and anxiety she had been feeling all morning. But before she could speak, she found herself tumbled lightly down across his thighs as he seated himself on the sofa. His golden brown eyes gleamed with a trace of his indulgent humor, but they also reflected the depths of his inflexible will. Abby felt a kind of puzzled wonder as she tried to comprehend the man who cradled her.

"You're serious, aren't you?"

"As you've pointed out, I'm always serious. Abby, I don't get involved in anything I don't wish to be involved in. But once I've made the decision..." He shrugged with massive finality. The message was clear.

"I used to watch in amazement as you made those flowers do exactly as you wished in class," she murmured, searching his face for answers to unknown questions.

"Just remember that I never bruised or broke one in the process." He toyed with several tendrils of her honey-eyed hair. "Abby, are you sleeping with that man in the photograph?"

"No."

"Did you go away with him this past winter? Did you sleep with him then?"

"Would it matter?"

"No. Not if it's all over between the two of you now. If it isn't, I want it over. And I'm willing to do the job if you're afraid to face him and tell him."

She watched him a moment longer and then she came to a decision. "I'm not having an affair with Ward Tyson, nor did I ever have one with him. He's my cousin's husband. Cynthia and I were practically raised together. We're like sisters. I wouldn't hurt her for the world!"

He assimilated that, his expression unreadable. "So what's the problem?"

"The problem is that . . ." She paused, licked her dry lips and tried again. "The problem is that there was a weekend a couple of months ago. A weekend that could be misinterpreted. It would hurt my cousin very badly if she were to find out about it. And someone else seems to know about that weekend."

"And?"

She couldn't tell how much he believed and how much he was simply filing away for reference. Without a word she freed herself and got up to cross the room to where her purse lay on an end table. She opened the red leather bag and removed the second photo along with the typewritten message. Silently she walked over to where he sat waiting and handed him the two items.

He studied them both for a tense moment and then put them carefully down on the smoked-glass coffee table.

"You're being blackmailed," he said quietly.

Hearing the word said aloud made her shiver. Unconsciously Abby crossed her arms over her small breasts in a childish gesture of self-protection. "It looks like it."

"How much?"

"I don't know yet."

"Any idea who?"

She shook her head, squeezing her eyes shut in despair.

"Where were you going when I arrived?" The questions weren't brutal, merely unrelenting. Abby was already regretting her decision to tell him the truth.

"Somewhere. Anywhere. I just wanted to get out of town. That second photo and the note arrived early this morning. All I've been able to think about for the past few hours is getting away from this apartment. I need time. Time to think. Time to draw whoever it is out into the open where I can deal with him."

"You're sure it's a him?"

"No, I'm not even sure of that. But I thought that whoever it is would try to find me and in the process I might discover who was making the threats."

"Did you think about going to the police?" he asked calmly.

"No!" She swung around to face him. "No, not yet. Not until I've had a chance to deal with it on my own.

I don't want Cynthia hurt unless there's absolutely no alternative. She's going to be crushed if she sees those pictures and someone tells her I had a fling with her husband! Oh, Torr, I can't do that to her. We're so close to each other. I don't want her hurt. I'll do anything to prevent that."

"Including paying off a blackmailer?"

"There must be a way of stopping him!"

"Or her," Torr reminded her mildly.

"Or her," Abby agreed bleakly.

There was silence in the room as Torr contemplated the information she had supplied. He had his answers now, Abby thought uneasily. What would his reaction be? For the life of her she couldn't read his hard face. The amber eyes were clear and steady but as unfathomable as always as he watched her tense expression.

"All right," Torr finally said.

Abby stared at him blankly. He had obviously come to a decision but she was helpless to guess what it might be. "All right, what?"

"If you want to make a run for it and see who follows, I'll let you."

She flinched, a little taken aback. Somehow, after demanding all those explanations, she hadn't expected Torr to simply withdraw and let her resume her plans. Was he going to abandon her now? Why had she let him force her into telling him the whole story? Proudly she tilted her head.

"Goodbye, then, Torr. You've detained me long enough."

One of the rare flashes of humor lit his amber eyes. "Detained you? Lady, that's only the beginning. My next step is to kidnap you. Since you're all packed and ready I guess there's no point hanging around. Let's go."

"What? Go where? Torr, what are you talking about?" she demanded seethingly, torn between relief and sheer outrage.

"You want to disappear for a while and see who comes looking, right? Well, I've got a place you can disappear to. I'll be along to help look over your shoulder so we don't get taken by surprise by whoever's sending you these." He scooped up the photograph and the note and got to his feet. When Abby failed to move he frowned warningly. "Don't dawdle, honey. We've got a long drive ahead of us."

4

ABBY SAT TENSE and withdrawn as Torr guided the BMW out of Portland going east along the interstate that paralleled the mighty Columbia River. For several miles the river formed the border between the states of Washington and Oregon, cutting a majestic swath through a spectacular gorge. The densely forested mountains rose skyward on Abby's right and the river surged toward the ocean on her left. It was a wonderfully scenic route and at any other time she would have been thoroughly enjoying herself. But today being on the floor of the gorge gave her a sensation of being trapped.

Or perhaps it was the knowledge that she was confined in a car with a man she barely knew, a man who was trying to take over her life, that gave her the trapped sensation.

Then again, maybe being a victim of blackmail always made you feel that way. Her fingers clenched into a knot in her lap.

"I'd tell you to stop worrying except that I don't think the advice would do much good," Torr mused as he glanced at her hands.

"You're right. I've never been in a situation like this in my life. I'm furious and I'm scared and I feel so awfully helpless. What if my idea doesn't work?"

"Oh, I think whoever it is will follow you. We left enough of a trail. Between meeting your neighbor in the hall and leaving a message with my answering service, it should be easy enough for anyone to figure out we're at my cabin near the Columbia River gorge. We didn't exactly make a secret of our exit."

Abby chewed on her lower lip, remembering the conversational way Torr had told her neighbor they were off on a trip. Mrs. Hammond's alert gaze had flashed to Abby and then back to the solid dark-haired man who stood by her side holding a suitcase.

"Excellent idea, if you ask me," Mrs. Hammond had volunteered. "I'm nearly eighty years old and I can tell you right now that if I had the first thirty years to do over again, I'd make a few interesting memories for myself. Have a good time, Abby dear. He looks like he can take care of you." The tiny woman beamed up at Torr. "Don't let her scare you off, young man. She's really much softer than she makes out at times."

"I'll keep that in mind," Torr had murmured obligingly.

"Lovely day for a drive," Mrs. Hammond had said, beaming.

"We thought we'd head for my place overlooking the Columbia."

"Up near the gorge? Wonderful country!" Mrs. Hammond had enthused. "Whereabouts?"

Torr had smoothly given the name of a small community and smiled blandly at Abby. "Ready to go?"

"Yes." Impulsively Abby had turned toward the older woman. "Mrs. Hammond, I wonder if you . . ."

"Don't worry about your plants, dear. Between Bonny Wilkins and myself we'll see to them. Run along now."

And Abby had allowed herself to be escorted into the elevator and out to the waiting BMW. There had followed a quick stop to Torr's house, a stark modern structure that she'd had no time at all to investigate. Torr had packed a bag with his usual efficiency and they had been on their way before Abby had seen anything other than the coldly contemporary black-and-tan decor of the living room.

"Abby," Torr said, interrupting her thoughts. "The real problem isn't whether or not the blackmailer follows you and shows himself. The problem is dealing with him when he does."

"I know," she answered, sighing.

"What did you plan to do then?" Torr pressed gently.

"I don't know! Torr, I can't even imagine what the person could want from me. I mean, I'm reasonably successful but I'm certainly not rich. There is no way I could give the blackmailer huge amounts of money."

"If he or she is a small-time sort of blackmailer, the demands will probably be correspondingly small," Torr asserted, shrugging.

"You don't seem overly concerned about them," she accused.

"The size of the demands? I'm not. You're not going to pay off, so it really doesn't matter how big they are."

"I may have to pay him off until I find a way to stop him."

"No."

"Torr, I have to be logical about this. Paying the guy off for a while will give me time."

"Whatever happens, you won't pay him. I can't let you." Torr's gaze was fixed on the highway, his profile set in stone.

Abby drew a deep breath. "You will have nothing to say about it. If I decide that the best way to handle the situation is to make a payoff, I will do it. My cousin's happiness is at stake here and I will do whatever has to be done to protect her. I'm not interested in any of your macho stands against blackmailers."

"Honey, you can't pay him off," Torr explained gently. "Once he has his hooks in you it will only get worse. The reason I'm going along with you at this point is because I think it's logical to try and draw whoever it is out into the open. Knowing your enemy is always a rational policy. After that we act."

"We'll see," Abby declared mutinously, not liking the way he was assuming control of the situation. "Have you had a lot of experience with blackmailers?" she added tauntingly.

"I've had experience with vicious people. Same difference."

Abby's head snapped around to stare at him. "What vicious people?"

"It's a long story and I really don't feel like going into it at the moment."

"Well, I've had some experience with domineering men," Abby retorted, "and I've learned a few things in the process, too."

The faint shadow of a smile flickered at the edge of his mouth. "No, you didn't. If you had, you'd have treated me the way I intend to treat the blackmailer. You wouldn't have given an inch. But you've already made the first mistake in dealing with me. You've given more than an inch. So you're stuck with me."

"That's not very funny, Torr."

"Sorry. You're not the first to complain about my poor sense of humor. We serious types lead a difficult life." The faint smile disappeared altogether. "Someday I'm going to want to know all about him. You do realize that."

Abby tensed, knowing there was no sense pretending she didn't know he was referring to the man in her past who had made her so wary. "It's not something I discuss frequently."

"We won't discuss it frequently. Just once. Completely."

Abby sent him an angry glance. "The only thing I'm going to say about that mess is that I learned a lot from it."

"Such as?"

"Such as the fact that real dominance, real possessiveness is neither romantic nor thrilling. I also learned that jealousy is a sickness, not a sign of passion."

"Go on," he encouraged softly.

Realizing that she had already said far more than she intended, Abby took a grip on herself. She would not let her impulsiveness push her into confiding everything to a man she didn't yet know well. No one, not even Cynthia, knew the full story of Flynn Randolph. "It's over. I try not to think about it and I make it a point never to discuss it."

"Has he ever tried to get in touch with you since you ended the relationship?"

"No, thank heavens!"

"Where does he live?"

"Seattle." She frowned. "Torr, I've said I don't want to talk about this. I think we should be concentrating on the real problem at hand."

"The blackmailer? Not much we can do until he or she decides to pursue you. In a rural area like the one I'm taking you to today, it will be difficult for a stranger to remain totally hidden for long. To get to you he'll be forced to ask some questions, make some waves. Sooner or later we'll have him."

Abby heard the finality in his last words and stared at her companion. "You talk as if we'll be able to do something permanent about him."

"I'll think of something."

Abby stirred uneasily, wondering exactly what she had gotten into by allowing herself to be swept out of town like this. As the miles rolled past she finally settled down and began to think about what she'd done. Her present position was highly uncertain, to say the least, but on the other hand, there was something distinctly comforting in the knowledge that she was no longer facing the problem alone.

There was a strength in Torr Latimer that reassured rather than terrified a woman. Abby wasn't certain why she seemed to find that true but she acknowledged it was a fact. Torr was capable of blunt intimidation—she'd already witnessed that—but somehow it hadn't left her feeling frightened or anxious.

A woman had to be so careful, she reminded herself for the hundredth time. She must not let herself be confused by passion and desire. And there was an element of both in Torr Latimer's eyes. He wanted her. He'd made no secret about it. How much of his present protectiveness was merely a convenient device to seduce her, she wondered.

"What are you thinking?" Torr interrupted calmly.

"That I'm getting paranoid."

"I'd say you've got grounds. People who are being blackmailed have a right to a degree of paranoia."

She flicked him a speculative glance. "I wasn't worrying about that. I know I've got a right to be paranoid on that subject."

"You're getting paranoid about me?" he hazarded gently.

"A little."

He thought about that for a moment and then nodded. "You may have grounds for that, too."

"Must you say things like that?" she stormed. "Can't you see I'm nervous enough as it is? I can do without your weird brand of teasing."

"What makes you think I'm teasing?" He looked genuinely surprised at her conclusion.

"Thanks a lot! Go ahead—make me more nervous, anxious and upset than I already am. I don't know what ever possessed me to run off with you like this. I must have been out of my mind to agree to let you take me away. I should have gone ahead with my original plan."

"And wind up facing the whole thing alone?"

"It might have been better than spending every minute wondering whether or not you're going to pounce on me."

"Is that really what you're worrying about? Or are you afraid you might not try to dodge when I do decide to, er, pounce?"

"You're finding this whole thing quite amusing, aren't you?" Abby accused furiously.

"No. Not amusing. Intriguing, perhaps. A little risky, maybe, but not amusing," he responded quite soberly.

"Risky! For me or for you?"

"For both of us."

"I never asked you to take any risks on my behalf," she reminded him righteously.

"I wasn't referring to the risks involved in confronting the blackmailer. I was thinking about the chances you and I are taking with each other." His low graveled voice was almost bland in tone, as if he were discussing a purely academic matter, one of intellectual interest only.

Abby eyed him cautiously. "What chances are you taking?"

"The chance that I won't be able to let you go after I've made you mine," he admitted simply. "The chance that I'm going to be caught up in your crazy, undisciplined, off-the-wall way of doing things. I'm not used to dealing with a woman like you, Abby Lyndon. I'm feeling a bit like one of the flowers in your arrangements."

"Of all the ridiculous notions!" she breathed, unable to deny that a part of her was suddenly, deeply fascinated. "How do you imagine my flowers must feel?" she blurted before she could stop the question.

"A little confused, disoriented, but rather intrigued. Part of a chaotic situation that can't be fully understood, but which might be quite interesting."

"You're laughing at me," she groaned.

"No, I'm trying to reassure you."

"Are you, Torr? I don't think you're doing a very good job. I think I'm getting more paranoid by the minute."

"Are you really afraid of me, Abby?" he demanded softly.

She looked at the steady grip of his large hands on the wheel of the car and thought of how efficiently and smoothly he drove. Then she thought back to the disciplined, orderly arrangements of his flowers. And then she considered the effect he had on her physically. "I'll let you know when I finally make up my mind," she informed him tartly.

He smiled at that but said nothing.

The house on the cliff overlooked the wide river and an expanse of the surrounding scenery that was quite breathtaking. Somehow the location and the view didn't surprise Abby. She glanced around at the forested grounds before trailing behind Torr to the front door of the cedar cabin.

"You seem to like being up high and having a view," she remarked, vaguely aware that she was hesitant about following him into the house. It was as if every step she took, every move she made today, was bringing her closer to Torr's side. The feeling that things were happening much too fast and that the consequences might be irrevocable assailed her. Abby fought the uncomfortable sensation by taking her time surveying the scenery. She was unaware of the hint of defiance in her expression or of the unconsciously aggressive stance she had assumed.

Torr paused halfway to the front door, a suitcase in each hand, and looked at her. With her feet braced slightly apart, her hands on her hips and that determined expression in her eyes, she reminded him of a bright, brave, slightly arrogant poppy flower. But night was coming and poppies needed safe, secure places to fold their petals when the warmth of the sun was gone.

"Having a place that looks down on things gives me a feeling of security," Torr told her quietly. "I suppose that's why I made sure my place in Portland and the cabin here were built on hillsides. Come inside. It's getting chilly out here. I'll start a fire and we can have something to eat."

Abby swung around on her heel and met his eyes for a long moment. Going inside that cabin was going to change things, decide matters in some indefinable way. This man wanted to be her lover. He had already assumed the role of protector. Tonight she would be eating his food, sharing his fire, sleeping under his roof. The web around her seemed to thicken and tighten as she stood assimilating the probabilities of her future.

"It's too late, Abby. Much too late. Come inside, honey. You'll be safe here." Torr's words were soft and deeply persuasive, promising everything she needed.

For an instant longer Abby hesitated and then she shook off the feeling of being caught up in a spell. She was capable of handling Torr if it came to that. And it would be reassuring to know he was sharing the house with her tonight. His presence, she knew, would help to keep the fears and the worries at bay. The decision made, Abby summoned up a very brilliant smile and went over to the car.

"I'll get the sack of groceries we picked up at that convenience store," she called cheerfully, leaning down to lift it off the back seat of the BMW. A flash of color caught her eye as she glanced inside the paper bag. "You bought some flowers!" she exclaimed in surprise. A small bouquet of tiny yellow roses poked their heads out of a plastic wrapper. They were nestled alongside a bottle of wine and a carton of milk. "I didn't see you pick these up."

"There were a few bunches near the cashier's stand," Torr explained as he turned back to the door to insert a key. "I thought they might add something to dinner."

"Are you going to fry them or boil them?" she asked, grinning.

"It's not nice to pick on people who take life seriously," Torr admonished as he pushed open the door and picked up the suitcases. He nodded for her to step into the tiled hall ahead of him and, traces of the grin still on her mouth, Abby did so. She gazed around with interest.

The interior of the modern cedar home had a professionally rustic look, complete with heavy comfortable furniture and area rugs with beautiful patterns. The orderly discipline she associated with Torr was very evident. There were no leftover ashes in the fireplace, no aging magazines on the slatted coffee table, no unwashed cups on the round oak dining table.

The house had obviously been designed to take full advantage of the view. A wall of glass formed one side of the living room and dining room. With a woman's unerring instinct, Abby headed toward the kitchen with her sack of groceries.

"Oh, lovely! An island. I've always wanted an island in my kitchen." She set the sack down on the wooden butcher-block table, which stood in the center of the functional room.

"Is that what you call it? I thought it was some sort of dining table. But it always seemed the wrong height to eat off of. I thought of buying some stools for it but then I decided I still probably wouldn't use it."

"It's a worktable, not a dining table," Abby informed him with a laugh. "Didn't you know what it was when you ordered it?"

"I didn't order it. I just told the designer to fix the place up and told her how much she could spend. This was the result." He vaguely indicated the handsomely furnished interior. "I haven't used the place all that much since I bought it."

Abby considered that, not knowing how to respond. Had he not used the house often because he was too busy working or because he had other things to do most weekends? To cover her lack of conversation she delved into the sack and began removing items.

"Who gets to arrange the roses?" she quipped, holding them up for inspection.

"You can do it while I take these suitcases upstairs to the bedroom."

Abby went still, her head tipped slightly to one side. "Bedroom? Singular?"

He shrugged. "Bedrooms, plural, if that's what you want."

"It is."

"I was afraid it might be." He picked up the cases and started toward the staircase. "I'll be back down in a few minutes."

Abby watched him leave, absently aware of how easily he carried the two cases up the stairs. A strong man and strong in more than just one way. With him around she was finally able to relax, even joke a little. After the last photograph had arrived that morning, she hadn't believed she would be feeling so much more at ease this evening.

Opening cabinet doors, Abby quickly explored the kitchen until she found a large glass that looked as if it would hold the little yellow roses. She threw the flowers at random into the glass and was standing back to admire her handiwork when Torr returned.

"Mrs. Yamamoto would be shocked," he remarked, surveying the roses.

"Fortunately I'm not being graded tonight." Abby wrinkled her nose in mock defiance. "Unless you were planning on assigning a score?"

"Good Lord, no! To do that I would have to understand your style and intent, wouldn't I?"

"Are you saying you don't understand me?" That information interested her greatly for some reason.

"Not completely. Not yet. But I will, Abby. I intend to devote a lot of time and attention to understanding you." There wasn't a hint of a smile in his eyes now.

Abby turned toward the sink, a head of lettuce in her hand. "You make me nervous when you look so very serious, Torr."

"That's the last thing I want to do. But I suppose I do want you to take me seriously." He moved to stand behind her, not touching her. "You're in my care now, Abby. I want you to trust me completely. I want you to know that you can rely on me." His hand lifted to touch her honey-colored hair briefly. "And ultimately I want you to give yourself to me."

"Torr . . ."

"I'm not going to pounce, Abby. It's really not my style. Be honest. Can you see me actually pouncing?"

She heard the wistful amusement in his voice and felt an answering tug of humor. "You may have a point. You don't look like the pouncing type." More like the all-consuming overwhelming type, she amended silently. Hastily she searched for a bowl, using the small action as an excuse to step out of his reach. "You know, we're going to have to sit down and talk about just what I'm going to do if and when the blackmailer shows his hand again, Torr. What kind of leverage do I have against him? My first instincts this morning were to run and give myself some time to think, but what good is time going to do? The more I think about it, the more nervous I'm going to get."

"Then don't think about it. Not tonight. We'll talk about it in the morning." He stood like another island in the kitchen, occupying the middle of the floor and watching her intently as she busied herself with the meal. "Just remember that whatever happens, you won't be dealing with it alone. In the end, we may have to call in the police. You do realize that, don't you? As soon as we know who it is, have some idea of what he wants, and some proof of what's going on, we'll have to notify the authorities."

"No!" Abby swung around, her blue eyes wide with dismay. "That's the last thing I want!"

"That's what the blackmailer is counting on, honey. That's why blackmail works in the first place."

"Torr, you promised you'd help me."

"I will."

"Then that means you don't go to the police. If I can't trust you far enough to be sure you won't do that, then I'm leaving."

"Settle down, Abby. I wouldn't do anything without talking it over with you first. You have my word."

There was a quiet arrogance in his voice that told her far more than anything else that he abided by his word. Abby faced him a moment longer and then turned back to the salad. The situation was a precarious one in so many ways—not the least her relationship with this man. She was beginning to feel as if her world were turning slowly upside down, and the threat of losing control made her fumble a bit with the knife she had just picked up to use on the tomatoes.

"Maybe I'd better slice the tomatoes while you start the steaks," Torr suggested, taking the knife from her fingers. He studied her expression a moment longer and then smiled. "On second thought, I think I'll pour us both a glass of wine before we go any further with dinner."

HE HAD BEEN RIGHT about the wine, Abby decided a few hours later as she lay in bed and waited for sleep to arrive. A couple of glasses had taken the edge off her anxiety, enabling her to relax and even enjoy the meal. Or maybe she had managed that feat because of Torr's calm, insistent manner of handling everything from the conversation to building the fire. Whatever the reason, she had been able to take his advice and put off until morning any further discussion of the mess in which she found herself.

But now as she lay alone in the darkness, the fears began to resurface. It was true that she felt a measure of temporary safety here in Torr Latimer's home, but how long could that last? And what right did she have to burden Torr with her problems?

Of course, she had hardly involved him deliberately, Abby reminded herself wryly. The man had simply taken charge this afternoon and involved himself. She wondered idly if there was anything that could stop Torr once he had been put into motion. A flickering smile touched her mouth as she thought about that, but it faded quickly as other thoughts, more dangerous thoughts, intruded.

Who could have taken those photos? And what could the blackmailer possibly want for them? Perhaps, as Torr had suggested, he would merely demand a steady, draining payoff. The image of paying off a blackmailer for the next several years was enough to make Abby throw back the down-filled quilt and scramble out of bed in restless anger.

As she wandered to the window to gaze down on the meandering swatch of darkness, the Columbia River, she was glad she'd thought to bring along her warmest flannel nightgown. A chill was settling in the house as the night deepened. Perhaps it was purely psychological, Abby told herself grimly. Perhaps the chill was independent of the environment tonight. How had other blackmail victims felt when they had been confronted with the threats?

Angry, helpless, trapped. All those things and more. When she was near Torr, she could push the frightening emotions to the back of her mind, she realized. But when she was alone, as she was now, they began to creep back out of the dark closet where she had tried to confine them.

This morning her instincts had been to run but now she questioned what on earth that was going to accomplish. Would the blackmailer really follow and perhaps reveal himself? What would she do when he did? And who could it be? What did he want?

The questions became a flood, driving her away from the window and into a tense pacing that took her from one end of the beige-and-brown room to the other. Desperately she tried to focus on her surroundings. The bedroom had clearly been designed as a rather neutral guest room, suitable for either a male or a female visitor. Abby wondered what Torr's wife had been like. Had he loved her deeply? There was a sense of relief in knowing that she had never come to this cabin. She had died, apparently, before Torr had moved to Portland. Did he have other family or friends? He was such a quiet, such an *alone* man. She couldn't imagine him surrounded by chattering relatives or even chattering friends. She could, however, imagine him with a woman. Only too clearly!

Damn! Why had that weekend on the coast ever happened?

What was Torr doing now? Probably sleeping in the master bedroom down the hall. She'd had a brief glimpse into the room on the way to her own. Enough to ascertain that in his room the designer had not been particularly neutral. The woman had obviously had a fairly accurate understanding of her client. The huge bed was the focal point of serenely austere furnishings. The color scheme was one of sober blacks and browns, offset by the finely grained furniture and the red-gold hue of the walls. Yes, Abby could imagine Torr with a woman in that bedroom, crushing her softly in that heavy bed.

This was getting ridiculous, Abby decided aggressively. She wondered if she had brought any tablets of tryptophan along with her. The amino acid was reputedly good for inducing sleep. It sold like hotcakes for her. But she couldn't recall having packed any. What else was supposed to work well? Abby paused, thinking. A glass of milk, perhaps? The hell with that, Abby told herself resolutely. She distinctly recalled a beautiful little oak liquor cabinet in the living room. It probably contained a nice bottle of brandy. And a sip or two of brandy might just do the trick.

Trusting the long-sleeved flannel gown to act as a robe, Abby cautiously opened her door and listened for a moment before going out into the hall. The house was throbbing with silence. She padded quietly toward the staircase. There was no sound from Torr's room as she went past, but the door appeared to be slightly ajar. Reaching out, she pulled it softly shut so that he wouldn't hear her rummaging around downstairs.

The thought of raiding her host's liquor cabinet brought a rueful gleam to her eyes as Abby traipsed down the staircase to the living room. At any rate, the midnight sortie was at least taking her mind off other matters.

But the momentary amusement she felt at stealthily finding her way through the shadowed living room to the liquor cabinet faded as the same questions came back to haunt her.

Who had seen her with Ward that weekend at the coast? Why had she even stupidly gone in the first place? Who knew enough about her relationship to her cousin to sense that it could be played upon in a blackmail attempt?

Yes, she thought grimly as she knelt down and groped about in the cabinet for a small glass, that last question was a very interesting one. Who did know her well enough to realize she would do almost anything to protect her cousin Cynthia?

But the question brought no answers—merely more questions. Her fingers fumbled awkwardly and she realized just how nervous she really was. What shape was a brandy bottle? Which side of the cabinet would Torr most likely store it in? He was such a disciplined, methodical person. Surely the bottles would be in some sort of regimented order. Unfortunately she couldn't see well enough to read the labels in the dark cabinet.

"I think I have what you're looking for here."

Abby shot to her feet, whirling around as Torr's voice came from behind her in the darkness. "Oh, Torr!" As she stared, he stepped from the shadows near the window where he had been standing. Pale light from a weak moon gleamed briefly on his clothing. It was obvious he had not yet gone to bed. He still wore the conservative shirt and slacks he'd had on earlier. "I didn't see you," she whispered, feeling suddenly very shy and very tense.

"I know. But I saw you. I watched you glide down those stairs like a little ghost with your golden hair all nicely mussed. I wondered if you had come looking for me, but when you went to the liquor cabinet I decided I wasn't your goal." He held up the bottle in his hand. Abby could just barely make out the shape of it. "Come on over here and I'll give you what you want."

With sudden irritation, Abby knew the invitation wasn't just for a glass of brandy. It just wasn't going to be that simple. Nothing with Torr was that simple. Slowly she moved across the darkened room to stand in front of him, uncertain of herself and of the man in the shadows.

Without a word Torr took the little shot glass from her fingers and poured out a measure of brandy. Then he set down the bottle and picked up a small object that had been lying on the table nearby. He opened his hand and Abby saw one of the delicate little yellow roses lying on his palm.

"I was just sitting here thinking of you," Torr murmured. He held out the rose, waiting for her to take it.

Abby glanced down at the pale object cradled in his large hand and then she lifted her gaze, trying to read the expression in his amber eyes. She knew there was a gleaming hunger in those eyes; she could feel it reaching out to surround her.

"I never pounce, remember?" Torr waited with seemingly unlimited patience for her to accept the rose.

The hunger wasn't just in him, Abby realized. It was in her as well. Without a word she put out a hand and touched the rose on his palm.

With great strength and sureness, Torr's fingers closed around hers before she could remove the rose. And then slowly, inexorably, he drew her to him.

No, Torr Latimer didn't pounce, Abby thought fleetingly as she obeyed the masculine summons. He overwhelmed, cradled and engulfed. And tonight there seemed to be both passion and safety waiting for her in his crushing embrace.

5

SHE CAME INTO HIS ARMS without a whisper of protest. Torr felt his body tighten and harden at the promise of her. She was so very soft. Soft and warm and vibrantly alive beneath the prim little flower-spattered nightgown. For an hour he'd been sitting down here in the darkness, thinking of her, pondering the mystery of her and the depths of the desire in himself. He could not remember wanting a woman as badly as he'd been wanting Abby Lyndon.

She had been almost silent as she had padded down the hall, but his instincts had leapt into pulsing awareness when he'd sensed her pause outside his door. In that instant his blood had begun to run heavily in his veins. The possibility that she might have been heading for his room stilled his breath.

But she had continued on past his door after shutting it gently and Torr had forced himself to calm down. Now where would she go? The rose with which he had been toying seemed to be burning his fingers as he waited for the next soft sounds. When Abby had reached the bottom of the staircase and gone straight for the liquor cabinet, Torr had wanted to laugh. She was within a few feet of him and apparently after the same thing he'd been after an hour earlier. A little liquid sleep inducer.

The realization that she was almost within reach undid any of the sleep-promoting effects of the brandy he'd been drinking. And now she was in his arms. A heady sense of satisfaction and anticipation threatened to make him rush. It took all his willpower to slow himself down. This had to be done right. More importantly, it had to be done thoroughly, completely.

When it was over she would know that she belonged to him.

"Torr?" Her voice was a bare thread of sound. He could feel her tremble against him and the knowledge that she wanted him acted like the most incredible aphrodisiac. "Torr, I didn't come downstairs for this. I only wanted a little brandy. Something to help me sleep."

He smiled down at her, his hands seeking the contour of the small of her back. "You have a beautiful back, did you know that? Sleek and supple and very graceful. Like the stalk of a flower."

"Torr, I don't think this is a good idea. Things could get very complicated if we . . . if we do this." Her face was buried in his shoulder and Torr heard the uncertainty in her voice. She was as wary and nervous of him as ever, but at least she was no longer fighting it as she had in the beginning. Tonight she needed him, wanted him—perhaps even desired the protection he could offer.

"Things will only get simpler when we become lovers, Abby. They won't get more complicated. Trust me, honey. Let me give you what you need tonight. I'll take care of you, protect you. Just give yourself to me and forget about everything else."

Abby shuddered beneath the soothing, enticing onslaught of Torr's gentle words. They seemed to surround her, offering comfort and pleasure and security. His arms did the same in a far more tangible way. She could feel the strength in him, but it didn't frighten her. Instead she sensed the promise of safety within his embrace and she found herself nestling closer to the hard, lean planes of his body.

"Put your arms around me, Abby. Let me feel you holding me."

Instinctively she did as he commanded, unable to resist the soft order or her own wish to comply. She wanted him, Abby thought in wondering amazement. She really wanted him. The desire in her was unfamiliar and unsettling. Was it a function of her own fears and her need for reassurance? If so, it was startlingly vivid and strong. She'd never experienced such a rush of feminine hunger. The force of her own rising passion confused her.

"Torr, I can't seem to think straight. I need a little time," she mumbled into the fabric of his shirt. "Please let me have a little time."

"Time won't make any difference in the way either of us feels. You know that. Tonight, tomorrow night or next week—it will be the same between us. It would have been like this the first night I'd met you if we'd allowed ourselves to step over all the barriers."

She sighed, an awareness as old as time telling her he was right. There was no point in even trying to resist this man. He offered everything she needed tonight. What was so wrong or dangerous about accepting what he had to give?

"Torr, in the morning . . ."

"In the morning we can talk," he assured her as his fingers sank heavily into the curve of her thigh.

"Yes."

"Right now I can only think about the way you feel under my hands. I want you, sweetheart. Can't you feel what you're doing to me?" He caught one of her hands and trapped it against his chest. When she raised her head to look up at him with wide, questing eyes, Torr covered her mouth with his own.

As always, his kiss overwhelmed and claimed. Abby felt his tongue thrusting between her lips before she'd even had a chance to adjust to the pressure of his mouth on hers. There was a soft sound, tiny and primitive. The cry of a female animal accepting the advances of her mate.

Torr reacted to it with a heavy answering groan of desire and he pushed her hand down his chest, over the flat plane of his stomach to the aggressive shape of his manhood. Abby caught her breath at the unmistakable readiness of him. Her senses swam as she tried to assimilate the potential ramifications of what was happening, but all she could think about was the compulsion she felt to surrender.

Beneath the fabric of his clothing Torr was aroused and ready. Abby wanted to satisfy that arousal. More than that, she wanted to be the only woman who could satisfy him.

"Abby, honey, I need you tonight." Torr pulled his mouth from hers long enough to explore the line of her throat. His fingers moved up her spine to the back of her head and then burrowed beneath the tangle of honeyed hair to find the sensitive nape of her neck.

"Oh, Torr, *please!*" Eyes closed against the exquisite pleasure of his touch, Abby leaned more heavily into Torr's waiting body.

"Just let go, honey. Let go and I'll take care of everything."

Torr feathered her lashes with his warm breath as he let his fingers trail lightly around her throat. His searching touch found the buttons on the front of the flannel nightgown and he undid the first with great sureness.

Abby gasped at the knowledge that matters were now drifting well beyond her control. In a small gesture of belated denial she covered his hands with hers and in the process dropped the yellow rose, which she had been clutching in the fingers of her right hand. It fell unheeded to the floor.

"Sweetheart, I'm going to make love to you tonight. Don't try to stop me. We both know now that stopping wouldn't be what either of us wants." As if her hands were gossamer, Torr slipped his fingers down to the next button of the gown, unfastening it easily.

She was acting crazily, she knew, and suddenly ceased her small efforts at restraint. She wanted him. There was no need to fight any longer. She felt him find the last button and then he was pushing the flannel gown off her shoulders, letting it drop slowly to her waist.

Any uncertainty she felt about how he would react to the sight of her body vanished beneath the heat of Torr's molten eyes. For a long moment he gazed down at her as she stood half-naked in the shadows, and then his fingers went to the tip-tilted crests of her breasts.

"Abby, you make my head spin. I feel as if I'm on fire," Torr breathed huskily. "On fire." His head lowered, his lips fastening on hers with such restrained ferocity that Abby shivered in response.

Excitement flared higher in her, making her senses shimmer. Her head followed the direction of his silent command, drifting back into the cradle of his shoulder as Torr caressed the gentle fullness of her breasts.

She could feel the ripening thrust of her nipples as surely as he must be able to feel it. Torr's soft growl of satisfaction told her that he was well aware of her body's response. Abby let her fingers trail along the column of his throat, slipping inside his shirt collar to find the first curling hairs on his chest.

For a moment longer Torr's palm grazed the hardening outline of her nipples and then with a sudden, unexpected movement his hand went down her stomach, catching the nightgown and pulling it off completely.

"Abby, Abby, honey, you're beautiful."

Torr let his hand hover for a moment just above the triangle of hair which defined the area of her womanhood and then he boldly pressed his fingers against her.

Abby cried out softly against his mouth, her body tensing with expectation and feminine uncertainty.

"Oh, sweetheart. Let me feel your warmth. I want you so, darling Abby. I need to know you want me."

The words poured over her skin and into her mouth as Torr's tongue tangled once again with her own. She could feel the probing roughness of his hand and the sensation sent ripples of shocked excitement through her. Her legs felt suddenly weak, unable to support her weight. When his foot thrust gently between her bare feet she gave way to his touch completely.

Instantly Torr explored her with incredibly enthralling intimacy. The feel of her seemed to release whatever bonds had been holding him until then.

"Ah, sweet Abby. So warm and welcoming. I'm going to lose myself in you tonight, sweetheart."

A moment later Abby felt the dark world revolve dizzyingly around her as Torr swept her up into his arms and started for the staircase.

"Look at you, woman," he teased huskily, "lying naked in my arms, your hair flowing down. You make me feel like some sort of conquering barbarian."

"Perhaps you are," she whispered, her eyes smoky now with the depths of her own desire and excitement. She felt him take the stairs with strong easy strides, her weight obviously not slowing him down. He carried her to the top and then turned unhesitatingly down the hall to the door of his own room. In another moment Abby was being settled in the middle of the wide, turned-back bed.

She lay watching him from beneath her lashes as he undressed in the darkness. Torr removed his clothes with an uncaring impatience, stripping them off and leaving them on the floor. When he turned to her, she found herself drinking in the sight of his magnificently aroused body, his obvious strength not at all intimidating here in the shadows. She should be wary of it, Abby thought distantly. She ought to be nervous now at the sight of him. But her arms reached up for him as he came down beside her and all fears were forgotten.

"Torr, I've never felt like this before," she confessed as he wrapped her close and snarled her legs with his own heavy ones.

"Neither have I," he admitted simply, and then he was sealing her mouth, crushing her back into the bedding.

He made love to her with a fiercely checked desire, as if he had to fight not to take her with sudden, ungovernable excitement. Abby flowered beneath his touch, turning to him as a daffodil turns toward the sun. The heat in him warmed her deliciously, making her feel marvelously alive. His response to her own initially tentative and then eager exploration thrilled her. She felt recklessly powerful, as only a woman can feel when a man she wants responds unhesitatingly.

Her fingers drifted tantalizingly over the contours of his strong back and Torr groaned aloud as she found his solid, muscled thigh.

"You make it so hard for me to do this right," he rasped, trembling violently as she stroked the inner side of his leg. His own fingers were even more mercilessly arousing, however, and Abby thought briefly that if anyone had a right to complain about not being able to slow down, it was she.

"Oh, Torr, touch me, yes, oh yes."

"Here?" he taunted gently. "Or here?"

"You seem to know exactly where. Oh, darling, *yes!*"

The pulsating excitement threatened now to take her by storm. She had to know the fullness of him inside her. The soft, feminine sounds in the back of her throat came more quickly and Torr drank them eagerly.

"Please, Torr." Her body lifted pleadingly against his hand.

"I want it to be perfect," he protested softly, teasing her with his touch until she was reaching out to urge him closer.

"It couldn't be more perfect. Torr, please take me. Take me now. I'm going out of my mind."

"I think that's how I want you this first time," he growled. "Out of your mind with needing me. Because you sure as hell have me out of mine!"

As if he'd reached the end of his self-control, Torr moved abruptly, crowding Abby back into the pillows with the weight of his body. She knew a sudden unexpected flash of tension, a primitive resistance that was almost as strong as the desire she felt. This was not merely a night of passion that could be somehow ignored in the morning. She was giving herself to this man.

Torr was aware of the brief panic in her almost before she identified it in herself and he moved to swamp it. "It's too late, Abby. There's no going back. I'm going to make you mine now."

The words were like sandpaper against the skin of her shoulder and then Abby couldn't think at all. Torr was lodging himself between her thighs, forcing her to accept his strong muscled body against her softness. Abby cried out in an agony of need, her arms wrapping him close as she obeyed his urgent summons. He was probing her, testing his strength against her, and then with a harsh thick groan Torr was inside her.

The stunning power of his possession took Abby by surprise, even though all her senses had been pleading for it. She felt as if she had been engulfed by a wave, half-drowned in the raging force of their combined passion. It was unlike anything she had ever experienced and she gave herself up to it because there was no alternative. In that moment, Abby knew she would have done anything to satisfy this man. Giving herself to him seemed right and perfect. In turn, she found herself taking. Her legs closed tightly around his waist and her nails left small half-moons in the flesh of his back.

"Yes, sweetheart, yes!" Torr drove himself into her again and again, filling her completely as he sought to quench the fire that flamed in both of them. He was losing himself, finding himself. The words that came to his lips were incoherent yet carried the most fundamental of meanings. The liquid velvet of her sheathed him tightly until he thought he would drown. He had known from the beginning that it would be like this. Unique. Perfect. Unbearably fulfilling.

When the ripples of completion swept through her, Torr felt them as an extension of his own pleasure; he knew a violent satisfaction at having been able to bring Abby to this level of sensation. He lifted his head with an effort, determined to witness every nuance of her expression in that moment. But he was too caught up in the final release to spend more than a few seconds enjoying her wet parted lips, tightly closed eyes and soft quick breaths. Knowing she was climaxing beneath him sent him over the edge. He didn't hear the rough exclamation that came from his own throat, but he was well aware of the fierceness of his release.

It was a long time later before Abby felt Torr reluctantly, slowly, unlock himself from her body. She opened her eyes to find him propped on his elbow, looking down at her with an infinitely disturbing expression in the depths of his amber gaze. She lay still, aware of his palm flattened possessively on her stomach and of the weight of his ankle chaining hers. The air around them was thick with the musky scent of their lovemaking and there was a dampness on both their bodies. The intimacy of the moment was overpowering.

"I've been wanting you like this for days," Torr said softly. "But even in my imagination I didn't realize how it would be." He shook his head as if a little dazed. "Nothing was ever like this."

"No," she agreed, aware that there was no point trying to hide her feelings in the rawness of the moment. "Nothing was ever like this. Oh, Torr, I've never felt . . . I've never known anything like this." Her eyes were wide with the brave honesty of that statement.

He lifted his fingers from her stomach and tenderly pushed back a strand of honeyed hair that lay damply on her cheek. "No woman has ever given herself to me so completely. You belong to me now, sweetheart. Do you realize that? You're mine. I think you were meant to be mine all along. But even if it wasn't ordained, it's a fact now. I'm going to take care of you, honey. I promise you that."

Abby lowered her lashes slowly, aware for the first time of the way the coolness of the room was starting to chill her perspiration-damp body. "Torr, I think I know what you're trying to say and I...I appreciate it, but..."

"Appreciate it!" he mocked gently, humor lighting his eyes for a second. "How gracious of you."

Abby looked up into his face again, her own expression not mirroring any answering amusement. This was serious for her and she had to make him understand. "I know that in the aftermath...I mean I understand that at times like this, people often say things they think are romantic. Men like to talk about women belonging to them and...and..."

"Considering the fact that I'm quite sure you haven't had a lot of experience conducting conversations at times like this, I don't see how you can set yourself up as an authority on what is and is not a common topic." The lazy amusement in him grew stronger and Abby was about to press her point when she realized what he'd just said. It sidetracked her.

"What do you mean you don't think I've got much experience in these matters?"

He leaned down and brushed her lips with vaguely arrogant assurance. "Have you?" he taunted lightly.

"Well, no, but I don't see how you can be so certain of that!" she muttered, taken off guard by his unexpected perception.

"There is something about you when you lie in my arms. Something soft and vulnerable and honest. I don't know how to describe it, but I do know that you couldn't be in the habit of doing this very frequently. If you were, you would have learned how to protect yourself emotionally. You would not be so sweet and giving. And there would not have been that moment of fear just before I took you," he added. The tightening of his fingers on her skin told her he had been aware of her emotions at that point.

The fact that he had read her so well was unnerving. It sent a flicker of apprehension down Abby's spine. Her eyebrows drew together in an intent expression as she tried to get back to the original point she wanted to make. Darned if she was going to lie here and give him the satisfaction of telling her just how little experience she'd had! The man was arrogant enough as it was.

"Torr, what I was trying to say before you diverted me is that I wish you wouldn't talk in terms of possession. It makes me nervous. I know that to you it's probably just a word, but to me it brings back reminders of how unpleasant a man can make life for a woman."

"You don't like the idea of being possessed by me? Not even now after what we've shared?" He drew his hand along the length of her thigh with a proprietary touch.

"It's sweet of you to talk of protection," she countered placatingly. "But please don't talk of possession. All right?" She brushed his mouth with a fingertip, trying to soothe the trace of rigidity that was threatening there. "Talk to me of flowers and being together and how you want me. I won't even mind if you point out just how much you can make me want you," she said with a whimsical smile.

"Not saying the words doesn't change my feelings. You belong to me now, sweetheart."

Abby shook her head once. "I belong to no one except myself, Torr. If you can't accept that, then whatever we have between us ends here now."

"Don't be afraid of me, honey. Please don't." The plea was husky and low as Torr bent to kiss her shoulder. "Just relax. If it makes you so anxious, we won't talk about it tonight."

"We won't talk of it ever," she said with quiet emphasis, aware of the stirring in her body as Torr began to trail his fingers slowly across her stomach. Where had he learned such magic, she wondered fleetingly. He only had to touch her and she seemed to burn.

"We won't talk of it until later," Torr told her firmly. "When you're ready to accept our relationship for what it is. But there is something else we do have to discuss. And I don't think it can wait any longer than morning."

"What do you mean?"

"I have to know about that weekend. I have to know why you were there with your cousin's husband in such compromising circumstances. I need to know what kind of hold the blackmailer really has on you. You can't expect me to keep working without all the facts."

Abby moved restlessly, twisting a little as though to slip out from under his caressing hand. She did not want to talk about what had happened that weekend. Not with anyone. Torr's hand somehow seemed to clamp around her waist, making it impossible for her to slide out of reach.

"Nothing happened that matters during that weekend, Torr," Abby told him very steadily. "It was a mistake. It's over and done."

"Did you spend the weekend with your cousin's husband?"

"I've already told you I didn't have an affair with Ward."

"But you did spend that one weekend with him? Does the blackmailer have something to hold against you? Why were you coming out of a hotel room with Ward Tyson? What was that weekend really all about?"

The questions came at her like the flicks of a whip, not quite violent but holding the promise of violence. Abby froze, the incipient passion fading in her body.

"Oh, honey," Torr muttered, immediately aware of the tightening of her beneath his hand. "I only want to know the truth. I have to know everything if I'm going to help you. Can't you understand that?"

"You were the one who insisted on helping me. I never asked for your assistance!"

He leaned forward, his mouth hovering just above hers. "Whether you asked for it or not, you've got it. The questions can wait until morning. Put your arms around me, Abby, and make love to me. I need you tonight."

She hesitated, unwilling to take the risk of surrender now that she knew he was going to request answers she did not want to give. But Torr allowed her no further opportunity to resist. He lowered himself along the length of her, his mouth moving hotly on hers as his hands stroked her body to readiness. In a matter of moments, she willingly pushed everything from her mind except the demands he was making on her and the equally fierce demands of her own body. The magic of their passion consumed them both.

ABBY AWOKE the next morning feeling a little angry, a little defiant and very much trapped. And for the first time since the blackmail had begun, the reason for her feelings wasn't that she had been made a victim of extortion.

She awoke with the knowledge that she owed Torr Latimer some answers. Abby didn't like the idea of owing a man anything, but she felt especially strange about the obligation she now felt to tell Torr the full truth.

How had she gotten herself into this situation? Frowning furiously, Abby pushed back the quilt and eased herself out of the huge bed. Torr slept on beside her, apparently oblivious of her uncertain temper. Abby paused beside the bed, surveying the man who had freed her passions so easily during the night.

She had admitted the truth when she'd told him she'd never known anything as extravagantly exciting and enthralling as his lovemaking. She had never realized just how much pleasure her body was capable of receiving—and creating. It was true her previous experience had been extremely limited, but Abby realized with sure intuition that she would never know with any other man what she had known with Torr the night before. Not even if she lived to be a lively old lady with a hundred passionate affairs behind her.

In fact, this morning, Abby thought gloomily, she couldn't even imagine having a hundred passionate affairs. She could only visualize herself in bed with one particular man. Torr Latimer.

Her mouth twisted in wry disgust as she stalked to his closet and pushed back the door to peruse the neat interior. There on a hook hung what she needed, a short terry-cloth robe. Yanking it down she wrapped it around her, the oversize garment nearly engulfing her. Then, with one backward glance at a still-sleeping Torr, Abby hurried out the door and down the hall to the sanctuary of her own bedroom.

There she sank wearily down onto her rumpled bed and contemplated her situation. Had she really expected to be able to go to bed with Torr, she asked silently, and not wake up to find herself bound to him.

The fact was, she hadn't given the future much thought at all the previous night. She had reached out to take the yellow rose from Torr's hand and found herself chained. From the instant she had grasped the rose she had been caught. No, perhaps it had been earlier than that. Perhaps it had happened the moment she had succumbed to his offer of protection. Or had it been the night she had let him drive her home from the class in flower arranging? The first time she had spoken to him?

It was disturbing to realize that she couldn't even pinpoint the moment when she would still have been free to walk away. Looking back, it seemed as if her relationship with Torr had been inevitable from the start. And everything that had happened since that first night in class had been a continuum of events, each inseparable from the one before, culminating in last night's ultimate commitment.

Was that what it was? A commitment? Had she really taken such a step so mindlessly with a man she hardly knew? It was incredible. Impossible to believe. But Abby couldn't shake the knowledge.

Restlessly she removed Torr's terry-cloth robe, aware of the intimacy she experienced just by wearing something of his. The garment undoubtedly fit his solidly muscled body perfectly, but on her it enveloped and overwhelmed. Just like its owner.

Letting it drop to the floor, Abby padded naked to the bathroom. The intent scowl on her face reflected severely back at her from the wide mirror over the washbasin. Her hair was a honeyed tangle and her body still looked warm and rosy from sleep. Her body didn't exactly *feel* warm and rosy from sleep, however. It felt alert and aware and just a little sore in places. Abby groaned to herself as she turned on the shower and stepped beneath the pulsating spray.

The feeling of being rushed into an affair she wasn't at all certain she wanted brought on a momentary sense of panic. Last night had happened much too quickly. She had too many other problems to deal with at the moment and she couldn't risk getting so deeply involved with Torr Latimer.

The problem was, Abby thought grimly, she already was involved. She needed to put some distance between them and give herself some breathing room.

Down the hall Torr stretched widely as he heard the shower go on in Abby's bathroom. He'd been aware of her leaving the warm bed a few minutes earlier, but he'd also sensed her precarious mood. Judging it best not to confront her first thing with the intimacy of the night, he'd allowed her to escape. In her usual impulsive, undisciplined fashion she'd fled his bedroom in order to give herself a chance to think.

That was all right with him. She wasn't going any farther than her own room and he couldn't deny her a little time to herself. She needed it to adjust to the situation, he decided, feeling indulgent. Everything had happened fairly quickly and she had a lot on her mind.

Not that anything would be changed when she finally emerged to face him, he added silently as he walked naked into his own bathroom. God, he felt good. Strong and alive and determined. Abby had made him feel this way. She was everything he'd ever wanted or needed in a woman. And she was his.

It was only a matter of time before she acknowledged that.

Abby dressed in a pair of faded, skintight jeans with a heavy leather belt that gave her a reassuring sense of machismo. It wasn't just men who could experience that sort of thing, she told herself as she tucked in the tails of a plaid shirt with a button-down collar. This morning she needed some of her natural self-confidence, and the belt helped for some reason. Made her feel a little brash and a little tough. Necessary qualities for going up against a man like Torr Latimer. She pinned her hair up into a semineat knot and headed resolutely downstairs.

Torr was sitting comfortably at the breakfast table, gazing out the window at a barge making its ponderous way up the Columbia when Abby walked into the room. He turned at once with a slow, intimate smile. In the morning sunlight streaming into the kitchen, he looked very real and disturbingly sure of himself, she thought. His black hair still gleamed from the shower and Abby remembered the feel of it. The dark slacks and open-throated white shirt he wore seemed to emphasize the flat clean lines of his body, rather than conceal them. His amber eyes were full of possession and memories and Abby suddenly realized that the bit of swagger she'd tried for with the leather belt was as nothing compared to the sure masculinity that emanated from this man.

"Coffee?" He got to his feet and went to the counter to pour a cup without waiting for her nod of confirmation.

Abby watched his smooth economical movements, aware of the images flitting through her mind—images of the night before when every movement Torr had made seemed to provoke a response from her body. When he handed the cup of coffee to her, she remembered the way he had offered the rose.

"Thank you," she managed almost formally and could have bitten her lip. This was ridiculous. She was no tongue-tied teenybopper unable to deal with awkward situations. Unconsciously her chin lifted and she met Torr's eyes with a grim boldness. "About last night," she began sternly.

"I have a suggestion to make about last night," Torr interrupted calmly, reseating himself. "I suggest we don't discuss it this morning."

"We have to discuss it."

"Not now. We have other matters to talk about this morning. Sit down, honey, and tell me about that weekend with Ward Tyson."

"Not before we discuss last night!" Abby exploded. She dropped into the seat across from him.

Torr gave her a small, surprisingly wicked grin. "Was last night more important than the weekend with Tyson?"

"Yes! I mean no. Now wait a minute, Torr, you're deliberately trying to confuse me. They're two separate issues and I want to settle last night first. To begin with, I want to make it clear that what happened last night is not the beginning of a routine affair."

"No affair with you would ever be routine."

"I want it understood that I'm not going to sleep with you on a regular basis," she ground out.

"Meaning you're not going to sleep with me tonight?" he asked whimsically.

"Exactly!" she shot back triumphantly. Why she should feel quite so much triumph wasn't clear. "Or tomorrow night."

"Okay. Now about Tyson."

"Torr, you're ignoring me!" She leaned forward, her elbows aggressively on the table.

"I could never ignore you, Abby. You're about all I think of these days," he countered with unnerving gentleness. "I'm simply going on to the next subject on the list."

"No arguments about the first subject?" she demanded.

"No arguments. I realize you need a little time."

"That's very gracious of you," she muttered, not at all certain of his mood.

"I can afford to be gracious at this stage. You aren't going anywhere and a couple of days isn't going to make much difference in the long run. Nothing will be changed. I can be reasonably patient."

"You mean that you're sure I'll come scurrying back to your bed once I've settled down and had a chance to think it all over?" she challenged coolly.

The whimsy died in his eyes to be replaced by great certainty. "Abby, you and I belong together. You're mine. Nothing can change that. Now about Ward Tyson."

Abby sat staring at him for a second longer. Suddenly discussing that horrid weekend seemed far easier than dealing with the bonds Torr was trying to place on her.

6

"THAT WEEKEND was a mistake," Abby uttered, sitting back in her chair and sipping morosely at her coffee. Her eyes went to the barge, which was making steady progress on the river. Headed for wheat country, she decided, knowing that the river curved up into the rich wheat lands of eastern Washington.

"I assumed that from the start."

Abby's head snapped around as she threw him a simmering glare. He looked at her steadily for a long moment and it was she who glanced away first. Eyes once more on the barge, she went on carefully. "My cousin and her husband had been having... difficulties. Cynthia's pregnancy was a hard one. There were complications and the doctor insisted she take no chances. She spent most of the last couple of months off her feet. Unfortunately Ward was under a great deal of pressure at the time. He had just been named president, and the board was expecting miracles. The company had been having problems, as I told you the other night. Ward felt under the gun to provide the miracles expected of him. He was working sixteen hours a day and coming home to a wife who was under a tremendous amount of strain herself."

"A situation ready-made for quarrels, accusations and fears," Torr put in astutely.

"Well, yes. I was spending a lot of time up in Seattle trying to help out. Cynthia had a housekeeper, but that didn't compensate for the loneliness and the worry that something was going to go wrong with the pregnancy. She was spending a lot of time alone wondering what her husband was doing. She started imagining things."

"Things like other women?"

Abby shrugged. "Yes." She hesitated, trying to find words to describe the next part of the tale. "As I said, I was spending a couple of days a week in Seattle. I would sleep in Cynthia and Ward's spare bedroom when I spent the night and sometimes I'd still be up watching television or something when Ward would get home. With Cynthia asleep in bed and no one else to talk to, he would get a drink and unwind talking to me. It got to be a little too much of a habit, I guess."

"And then one evening he wanted to unwind with more than a drink and a little conversation, is that it?" There was a curious hardness in Torr's voice but he continued to drink his coffee quietly.

Abby stirred uneasily, remembering. "Ward is really a very nice man," she tried to explain.

"But he's a man."

"He was under a lot of strain."

"You're defending him for seducing you?" Torr asked far too mildly.

"He didn't seduce me!"

"He made a pass?"

"It . . . it was an awkward situation," she said sadly. "He'd been out to a business dinner that evening. Had a couple of drinks. When he got home he had a few more, saying he wanted to relax. He asked me to stay up and talk to him. He explained how depressed he was feeling, told me about his problems with the company and how hard things were with Cynthia. One thing led to another and . . ." Abby moved a hand vaguely in the air to explain the rest. Torr, however, refused to accept such an explanation.

"And what?"

"He tried to kiss me. Said he needed a woman and that he admired me very much. Felt I understood him and the strain he was under."

"Poor misunderstood corporate executive."

"If you're going to be snide about this I'll stop right now!"

"Don't stop now. We're just getting to the interesting part."

"Has anyone ever told you," Abby ground out, "that you're inclined to be rude, arrogant and overbearing?"

"You have. On several occasions. Let's get on with the story."

Abby thought of the variety of different responses ranging from pouring the remainder of her coffee over his dark head to stealing the BMW and making a quick escape. None of them seemed practical in view of the intent way he was watching her. And Abby realized she had come too far with the story to stop now.

"There was an embarrassing struggle. I managed to get to my bedroom and lock the door. He didn't try to follow and I assumed that was the end of it. But it made things very awkward the next day. I left for Portland. That coming weekend I had a long-standing arrangement to spend a couple of days on the coast."

"By yourself?"

"By myself," she affirmed coldly. "I take a lot of vacations on my own. I find it's much more pleasant than traveling with some man who expects me to warm his bed for him even though I'm paying my own way."

"All right, let's not get into that subject," Torr said soothingly. "I take it Tyson was aware you were going to the coast?"

"Yes, he and Cynthia both knew. I'd talked about it on a couple of occasions." Abby got up to pour herself some more coffee. She thought about not offering Torr any but didn't quite have the nerve to ignore him. Silently she refilled his cup and then sat down again. "I checked into my room that weekend and a couple of hours later there was a knock on the door."

"Tyson," Torr growled.

Abby nodded. "Ward had followed me to the resort. Claimed he needed the time away from the demands of a sick company and a sick wife. Said he knew I understood because of the way I had understood during all those long conversations we'd shared. I told him I wasn't interested in a weekend affair with him. Told him to go home to Cynthia and stop acting like an immature boy. I really read him the riot act."

"Because you were feeling a little guilty?"

"I suppose so. I began to wonder if I'd been leading him on by playing the role of confidante so many evenings. I felt terrible that it might be partly my fault he was acting as he was. It was all very difficult because I genuinely like Ward. I always have. And I did understand that he was under a lot of pressure trying to salvage the firm."

"But you sent him on his way back to Seattle?"

Abby nodded firmly. "What's more, by the time he left the following morning, he'd realized what a bad mistake he'd nearly made. He was regretting the whole thing."

"He stayed the night and left the next morning?" Torr persisted.

"Yes."

"He spent that night in his own room?"

"Yes!" she flared, annoyed at being pushed and prodded. "I had breakfast with him before he left the next morning and we talked it all over. He was as relieved as I was that nothing had actually happened. He felt terrible about having made the attempt."

"How did he explain the weekend to Cynthia?"

"How should I know? Probably told her he had an out-of-town business meeting. The baby was born soon after that and then everything was all right again between Ward and Cynthia. But if Cynthia ever saw those pictures, she'd know he lied about where he was that weekend, and thinking I was involved too would really crush her." Abby looked at him pleadingly. "I can't have her hurt like that, Torr. Even if I could convince her that nothing happened during that weekend, she'd always wonder about my true relationship with Ward. It would never be the same between myself and Cynthia."

"And someone knows that."

Abby took a deep breath. "Apparently so."

"We're going to have to start figuring out who would know you that well."

"That thought makes me very, very nervous, Torr," Abby said slowly. "Who do I know that would do such a thing?"

"I suppose it could be someone you don't really know but who is aware of your close relationship with Cynthia. I wonder if Tyson's getting the same treatment."

Abby shuddered. "Maybe I should talk to him. Tell him what's going on and find out if we're both getting the threats."

Torr got to his feet, amber eyes chilling. "If and when we approach Tyson, I'll handle him for you. The last thing I want is for the two of you to be drawn together by mutual adversity."

"Are you jealous, Torr?" she couldn't resist taunting. Abby was totally unprepared for the immediate response her crack drew. Torr, who had been in the process of opening the refrigerator door, abruptly released it to stride back across the kitchen. He reached down and pulled her to her feet, his hands hard on her arms.

"Is that what you want, Abby? To make me jealous?"

Abby instantly regretted her momentary urge to goad him. "You know it's not." She swallowed uncomfortably. "A display of jealousy is the last thing I want from any man." Memories of Flynn Randolph's rages flashed through her mind and were reflected in her blue eyes.

"Then I suggest you don't try to provoke me. Any man can be made jealous under the right circumstances and I'm no different than other men."

That got through to something deep inside Abby. She shook her head and a faint smile touched her mouth. "You're wrong, Torr. I think you are different from other men. If I didn't, I wouldn't have made love with you last night." She lifted her fingers to touch the rough side of his cheek. That much was the truth, she realized suddenly. And it made this morning much easier.

"Abby..." Torr caught her questing fingers, crushing them in his palm, and pulled her close. "Abby, honey, please don't fight me. Don't be afraid of me. And don't panic about what happened last night. I'll give you time, I swear."

She stood on tiptoe and brushed her mouth lightly across his. "Will you, Torr?"

"I think," he whispered huskily, "I'd give you just about anything you wanted except..."

"Except what?"

Your freedom, Torr finished savagely in his head. Fortunately he had the sense not to utter the incriminating words aloud. "When I decide where I'm going to draw the line, I'll let you know," he replied gently. "In the meantime, feel free to keep asking for whatever you want."

She looked up at him earnestly. "And what about you, Torr? What do you want?"

"Right now I want breakfast." With a smile he patted her tightly encased rear. "Want to flip a coin to see who gets to make it?"

"I'll make breakfast this morning if you'll do it tomorrow. How's that?" Abby asked cheerfully, tacitly admitting there would be a tomorrow.

"Fair enough, as long as you don't try to slip any of your vitamins into the scrambled eggs." Torr reached for the coffeepot.

"Judging from your performance last night," Abby heard herself say very daringly, "I don't think you need vitamins. Not even my specially fortified formula designed for the, uh, socially active male."

A slow smile lit Torr's eyes. It evolved quickly into a laughing, wicked, blatantly male expression that brought an answering flush to Abby's cheeks.

"How do you want your eggs?" she demanded, turning away to avoid the brilliant gleam in the amber gaze.

"The same way I want you. Any way I can get them."

THE EXQUISITELY tentative, fragile, budding relationship that had been initiated between Abby and Torr grew into an almost comfortable, surprisingly companionable truce during the next few days. Abby decided that the only way she could describe Torr's attitude toward her was cautious. He was careful not to make any references to the night they had spent together. He was careful not to give orders. He was careful not to push her back into bed. All in all, she realized, he was doing his best to make her relax around him. And it was working.

Torr was also doing his best to come up with some answers concerning the blackmailer. He had sat down with Abby and gone over a list of everyone she knew in Portland or Seattle who might be likely to blackmail her.

"Maybe it's someone Ward knows, not me," she suggested at one point, glowering at the useless list they had drawn up together.

Torr nodded reluctantly. "But then why hit on you? Why not blackmail Tyson?"

"Perhaps because whoever it is knew I'd be more vulnerable," Abby replied, sighing.

"Which brings us back to someone who knows you pretty well."

"Torr, I simply don't know anyone who would stoop to this sort of thing."

"Okay, okay, honey, calm down. We'll go back to work on the list later. What do you say we run down to the village and pick up some food and maybe a bottle of champagne?"

"What are we celebrating?"

"How about the last night of flower-arranging class?"

"Good heavens, that's tonight, isn't it? Oh well, I was flunking out anyway. A trip to the store sounds better than working on this list." She looked at him and smiled. "I get the feeling you're trying to distract me."

"I am." He stood up and reached for her hand.

"Consider yourself successful," she told him, grinning.

But the distraction proved exceedingly temporary. Torr had barely walked into the small grocery store that served the community when he was cheerfully greeted by the owner, Carla Ramsey. Carla, Abby had learned on her first visit, made it a point to keep track of the comings and goings of everyone who had a home or a cabin in the area. It was a hobby, the older woman had explained blithely.

"'Morning, Torr. Did your friend from Seattle find you?"

Abby felt Torr's sudden tension but his voice was casual. "Apparently not. Haven't had anyone come calling. Someone came looking for me recently?"

"Day before yesterday. I gave him surefire directions to your place, but maybe he couldn't find it after all." Carla winked at Abby. "Or maybe he just decided he didn't want to bother the two of you. I told him Torr wasn't alone."

Abby shivered, a thousand questions coming to her lips. Evidently Torr's own questions weren't far behind. He got his in first.

"What did he look like, Carla?" he asked as he deliberated over the frozen steaks. "Maybe I can figure out who it was and give him a call. Abby and I are fairly hospitable, aren't we, Abby?"

"Of course." Did anyone notice how thick the words sounded, she wondered.

"Hard to describe," Carla said. "Nice lookin' man about thirty-five or so, I'd say. Course, it's difficult to tell about age. Brown hair, I think. Kind of on the thin side. Wiry, you know." She shrugged. "Sorry, I never was much good at describing folks."

"I see," Torr said easily as if the matter were unimportant. "Could be anyone. Did you notice the car?"

"Just a Chevy. Nothing special. Light-colored, I think. Does that help?"

"Nope, but don't worry about it." Torr crushed Abby's hand in a reassuring fashion and then pushed her in the direction of the vegetable bin. "See what you can find for a salad, honey."

Abby obediently headed for the vegetables, almost unable to focus on the row of head lettuce. The blackmailer had been here. Right here in this store! It must have been him. At least they had confirmed that it was a him and not a her, she thought bleakly. But it was frightening to know the man had been this close, that he had tracked her this far. The illusion of safety she had been enjoying for the past few days disintegrated. Now the blackmailer knew about Torr. That realization made her fingers tremble as she blindly selected the lettuce.

By the time she reached the counter, Carla was assuring Torr that she had not only given the stranger accurate directions, but had really had quite a pleasant chat with him.

"A real friendly guy. Wanted to know how you were doing, how often you got to use the cabin. All kinds of things."

"I see." Torr affected mild interest while he glanced around for anything he might have forgotten. "Probably a business acquaintance who was just passing through. After you told him how to get to my place he must have decided he didn't have the time to look me up."

"Well, like I said," Carla smiled broadly, "once I told him about your friend Abby he probably decided he didn't want to intrude. Will that be all?"

"Yes, I think that will do it. Anything else, honey?" Torr glanced inquiringly at Abby, who barely managed a polite expression.

"No, there's nothing else we need for tonight, Torr."

He must have realized she was trembling because he grasped her arm very firmly in one hand while he scooped up the sack of groceries in the other. Torr took both of his packages outside to the BMW and deposited them. Abby didn't know about the grocery sack, but she was extremely grateful to be set down. Her knees had become distinctly wobbly.

"I think I need some calcium tablets," she muttered. "My legs feel quite weak. And maybe some more iron, too."

Torr slid into the driver's seat and reached out to grasp her firmly by the shoulders. "We don't know for certain it was him."

"It must have been."

"All right, I'll agree it most likely was him. But that doesn't mean you have to panic. It just means your plan to draw him out of hiding is working."

"He knows about you now, Torr," she whispered starkly, searching his face.

"So? That was part of the plan, remember?"

"Your plan. Not mine. I had no right to involve you in this." Oh, what had she been thinking of to let him help her? How could she possibly protect him? The thought of Torr being in danger because of her was suddenly an overwhelming burden.

"You didn't involve me. I involved myself. I practically kidnapped you, if you'll recall. Abby, don't you dare start in on a guilt trip because of me. If you so much as apologize for the situation we're in, I swear, I'll . . ." He snapped off abruptly.

"You'll what?" She tried a tentative smile and was surprised to find that it worked. There was something vastly reassuring about having Torr Latimer here beside her.

"I was going to threaten violence," he explained wryly, releasing her to start the car, "but then I decided that might not be quite what you need to hear under the circumstances."

Abby watched his controlled movements, vaguely aware of how much pleasure she took now in simply observing him. "I don't see you as the violent type," she decided, relaxing somewhat.

For some reason that drew an almost amazed reaction from him. Torr took his eyes off the winding road long enough to send her a disturbingly probing, almost fiercely demanding glance. "You don't?" His voice sounded unnaturally restrained.

"No."

"Remember that in the future, will you?"

"Why? Going to make more threats?" she asked lightly.

He shook his head impatiently, concentrating now on his driving. "Abby, I told you the other morning that any man could be made jealous under certain circumstances. Well, I think any man could become violent under certain circumstances, too."

"Human nature, I imagine," she remarked shrugging, wondering why he sounded so tense. "Male nature."

"Yes. But Abby, I want you to know that I would never hurt you."

She was deeply touched by his attempt to calm and comfort her. "I wouldn't still be here alone with you if

I thought you might be capable of turning violent with me," she said gently. It was the truth.

That didn't appear to have the desired effect. Torr's strong fingers tightened on the steering wheel and his mouth hardened. "I want you to trust me, Abby."

"I do." These past few days had built the foundation of that trust, she realized. Confidently she reached out to touch his sleeve. When he glanced quickly down at her hand she withdrew it.

"Do you really, Abby? Trust me completely, I mean?"

"Torr, why the inquisition? I've just told you I wouldn't be here with you now if I didn't. I wouldn't have let myself be kidnapped from Portland if I hadn't felt on some level that I could trust you. The only thing I'm worried about at the moment is dragging you into my problems."

"I'm not giving you any choice on that score. I'm going to take care of you, Abby. That means I'm involved in your problems. Speaking of which, I think we ought to go over that list of yours with Carla's description in mind."

She sensed his desire to revert to a more businesslike topic and was about to go along when another thought occurred to her. "Torr, what about your work? How long can you be away from it?"

He appeared unconcerned. "As long as I want. I have nothing hanging fire at the moment. I'm not trading any contracts just now."

"No pork-belly futures going through the ceiling?" she teased.

"Actually, I made my profits in grain futures this past year," he told her. "The drought in the Midwest gave me an edge. I managed to buy contracts on corn before the prices started to climb."

"And made a bundle when everyone realized the harvest wasn't going to be so good this year, hmmm? There's something intriguing about that kind of speculation, but I think it would make a nervous wreck out of me. I'll stick to vitamins. Maybe I should try selling them to commodities traders. Sounds like the kind of business where people need to take their vitamins and minerals regularly."

"Knowing commodities traders, they'd probably try to find a way to trade them rather than take them. Abby, about that description of Carla's . . ."

She sighed and sank back into the depths of the leather seat. "Torr, it could be almost anyone. Even a couple of my salespeople."

"I thought most of your salespeople were women."

"They are, but I've got a few men, too."

"How on earth did you ever get into the door-to-door vitamin business, anyway?"

"By accident. Someone came to my door one day selling cosmetics and I decided that if people bought things that made them look good, they'd probably buy stuff that made them feel good. Especially here on the West Coast where everyone's so fitness-crazed. I was looking for a major career change at the time, so everything coincided nicely."

"I was in the same position myself when I decided to get into commodities trading," Torr said quietly. "I wanted a career change."

She had an urge to ask him more about that need, a part of her wondering if there had been personal considerations involved as there had been with her. But something held her back. There were private depths in Torr that she was not yet ready to plumb. For fear of being turned away? Perhaps. Or maybe for some other, unnamed fear. In any event the moment passed as Torr went back to the subject at hand.

"If Carla's visitor was our blackmailer, then he now knows where you are. He'll act on the information.

"Oh, God, what am I going to do if he comes knocking on the door with a gun or something?"

"He won't."

"You sound awfully certain of that."

"It makes sense for him to keep his identity a secret if he can. Why take the risk of having you possibly hire someone to get rid of him?"

"That's a thought!" What a splendid idea. Hire someone to get rid of whoever was blackmailing her!

"There's a slight drawback to hiring a professional remover of other people," Torr said dryly.

"Money? It would be worth the price!"

"For someone who's not big on violence, you're suddenly sounding rather ferocious. Do you realize exactly what you're saying?"

"It's just that for a moment there it sounded like such a neat plan."

"Not so neat when you consider the fact that you'd be left to deal with a professional killer after he'd done the job. If you think you've got trouble now, just imagine what that might be like."

"You're right, I suppose," Abby agreed, albeit slowly.

"Don't sound so forlorn. You've still got me, remember?"

"But we've just decided you're not the killer type," Abby pointed out ruefully. She waited for his answering smile and when it didn't come she found herself hurrying into conversation. "So, we're stuck with a description of a man who could look like anyone and who drives a car which could belong to anyone."

"We'll go back through that list of people you know when we get home. Not everyone on it is male, has brown hair and is wiry and thin. Surely we'll be able to eliminate a few!"

"We're not even sure the guy's on the list to begin with," Abby protested disgustedly.

"Even if he's not, he'll soon be making another move. When he does we'll probably have a few more clues with which to work. It's like watching the commodities market," Torr offered easily. "A couple of hints here and there, a little speculation and a lot of grass-roots psychology. Apply everything properly and you'll come out a winner."

"You sound so sure of yourself."

"I was trained to be," he answered, shrugging.

"In the commodities market?" she asked curiously.

"No. Before that. When I had another job."

He was closing up on her again, Abby realized, discouraging questions he didn't want to answer. This time she persisted. "What sort of job?"

"I worked for a large corporation up until almost three years ago," he told her shortly.

"And that's where you learned to be decisive?"

"Goes with the territory."

"I don't know about that. I think that with you it comes naturally," she said thoughtfully. He seemed quietly grateful that she let the subject drop.

THE BLACKMAILER didn't make his next move until three days later. Abby had begun to relax again. She had even gotten to the point of wondering if the knowledge that she was with Torr had discouraged the extortionist. Over breakfast one morning she brought up that possibility.

"Maybe he's been scared off now that he knows I'm not alone," she remarked, spreading red currant jelly on her toast.

"Maybe." Torr didn't appear convinced.

"After all, in the beginning he was only threatening one lone woman. The whole picture might have changed for him when you came into it."

Torr looked up from the copy of the *Wall Street Journal* he'd gone down to the village for earlier that morning. Something close to anticipation flared in his amber eyes. "In which case you'll have to stick close to me, won't you?"

Abby paused in the act of spreading the jelly and tilted her head to one side. It was suddenly borne in on her just how very domestic this little breakfast scene was. The knowledge made her feel uncomfortably warm. "Don't you think you might grow a little bored with a long-term arrangement like that?" she asked delicately.

Torr folded the *Journal* and placed it neatly beside his plate. Then he picked up his coffee cup and met her eyes over the brim. "No," he said quite simply.

"Oh." She couldn't think of anything else to say. There was a pregnant pause. Then she held out a slice of jelly-spread toast. "Want some more toast?" she asked with unnatural brightness.

"No, thank you."

She ate it herself in a rather large gulp that nearly choked her. A swallow of coffee overcame the obstacle.

"Abby," Torr asked gently, "do you really think I could take the thought of you having breakfast like this with some other man now that we've been together?"

She lowered her lashes uncertainly, aware of the ripple of excitement in her veins. "It's not as if we're having an . . . an affair," she pointed out weakly.

"We've slept together once," he said quietly. "It will happen again. In fact, it's going to happen on a very permanent basis one of these days. I'm only giving you a little breathing space at the moment."

"Gosh, thanks!" Her abrupt annoyance at his masculine arrogance blazed in her eyes. "As it happens, I'm very fond of both breathing and breathing space!"

He grinned unexpectedly. "Then enjoy yourself for the time being. One of these days you're going to run out of breathing room. And when you do, I'll be right behind you."

"You said you weren't the pouncing kind!"

"I'm not going to pounce. I'll just be there when you run out of breath."

"Sometimes you annoy me a great deal, Torr Latimer!"

"But I don't frighten you," he pointed out with serene satisfaction. "Not any longer."

He was right, she was forced to admit. He didn't frighten her. At least, not in the ways she had once been frightened of a man. Which was not to say she shouldn't remain wary of him, Abby told herself. Torr presented an entirely different sort of threat from the kind she had previously feared. Sometimes subtle, often teasingly blatant but always *there* was the inescapable knowledge that he wanted her, that he was waiting for her. The relationship between herself and Torr was complex in many ways and astoundingly simple in others. The attraction between them remained a carefully banked fire, but it was stronger than ever.

But while he kept the physical side of the relationship under control, Torr allowed companionship to grow stronger. She and Torr had become friends this past week, Abby realized at one point. It was a unique friendship, however. Not the easy casual association she normally allowed herself and a nonthreatening male, but a pulsing vital relationship that blended at the borders into an emotion she was still reluctant to name.

It had dawned on her slowly during their morning walks, which had become a daily ritual, that there was a growing sense of inevitability buried in her feelings toward Torr. In the back of her mind was the knowledge that it could be only a matter of time before good friends became lovers, especially when the physical attraction simmered so constantly beneath the surface.

It was during the after-breakfast walk on this particular morning that Abby found herself finally accepting that sense of inevitability. For the first time she stopped trying to repress the knowledge that if she stayed near him she was bound to run out of the breathing room Torr had promised. And for the first time she didn't allow that knowledge to feed her habitual caution.

Perhaps it was the serenity of their environment that allowed her to accept the dangerous situation between herself and Torr. The dark-haired man beside her seemed a part of that cool serenity. His fingers were laced with hers, strong and sure, as he guided her along one of the forested paths behind the cabin. It wasn't that he had the look of a backwoodsman or a lumberjack, she thought with a small secret smile. Rather Torr seemed in harmony with his surroundings, a counterpoint to the towering pines and the crunch of needles underfoot. There was a fundamental strength in him that reached out to envelop her just as the fresh, clean morning surrounded her. The temptation to surrender to both the vivid mountain day and the man who shared it with her was intoxicating.

"Tell me about him," Torr ordered gently as he led her to a clearing at the top of a crest overlooking the river. He wasn't watching her face, because his attention was on the dark swath of water below, but she knew he sensed her startled reaction.

"About whom?" The wariness that had faded to the back of her mind abruptly moved forward again.

"The man who made you so cautious. The one you say taught you to fear a man's possessiveness."

Abby sighed. "Why do you want to know about Flynn Randolph? Believe me, I do my best not to think about him."

Torr shook his head, sinking down onto the dry pine needles and tugging her down beside him. He smiled bleakly as she drew her jeaned knees up under her chin and wrapped her arms around her legs. "He's there in your head all the time. Whenever I get too close I can sense him. The only time I manage to drive him away is when I..." He stopped abruptly, his hand curling around a stray wildflower that had poked its bright yellow head up amid a patch of greenery.

But Abby knew what he had been about to say. "When you make love to me."

"Yes."

"I should think that would be enough to satisfy your ego." Instantly she regretted the words. She hadn't meant to snap at him, not on this soft fresh morning. The breeze lifted the tendrils of her honey-colored hair as Torr regarded her silently for a tense moment.

Then he leaned forward and brushed the small wildflower he had plucked against her lips. His mouth followed, taking hers in a short blatantly possessive kiss.

"It's not my ego that needs gratification at the moment," he told her calmly.

"What, then?" She could still feel the imprint of his hard mouth and the trace of the flower's softness. It left her warm and restless and a little hungry for something she didn't want to put into words.

"My curiosity. My sense of something being hidden. My need to know you completely." He let his hand fall from the nape of her neck. "I told you that you remind me of one of your own flower arrangements. A man has to keep examining you from all angles in order to figure out exactly what's involved. On one level everything seems relatively open and straightforward. But it doesn't take long before it becomes obvious there are a lot of hidden complexities. You fascinate me, honey. I want to keep peeling away the petals until I find the real you. So tell me about him."

"And if you don't like what you find?" she challenged huskily, her gaze on the traffic winding its way along the interstate that followed the river. The cars appeared very small from up here, just another species of animal migrating through the forest. The river and the gorge it had cut had been here eons before the cars had arrived and would undoubtedly remain long after the metallic creatures had disappeared from the earth. Some things were enduring and inevitable. In her world, Abby realized, Torr had become as much a force as the ancient river.

"I'm not worried about whether I'll like what I find beneath the petals," Torr said softly. "I've already satisfied myself about that. I just want to be sure that I drive out the shadows that other man left. I want to know every last petal is mine with no reservations."

There was no point trying to delay or lie. Torr had a right to know. Why he had that right Abby couldn't quite explain to herself, but she didn't argue further. "We worked for the same real-estate development firm in downtown Seattle," she began slowly. "Flynn was an executive. I was in sales. He was everything women generally find attractive in a man. Good-looking, successful and incredibly charming. When he took an interest in me I was thrilled. He made a perfect escort. Headwaiters all over town knew him by name. He always had tickets to the ballet or the theater. Going out with him was like going out on a date faultlessly orchestrated by a fairy godmother. I never had to make any decisions or even offer suggestions. Flynn handled everything. It took me a while to realize just how little input I had."

"And when you did realize that, he didn't want any suggestions?"

"He didn't take them well." Abby grimaced. "In fact, he got inordinately upset whenever I suggested we do something different than what he had planned. At first his masterfulness was rather intriguing. I felt pampered and special. But then it became annoying. He got angry when I tried to tell him what I wanted. He didn't make a joke out of it the way you did that night with the squid. He got genuinely furious. He had a reputation for losing his temper when he was thwarted in business, but because he was a man, people accepted that. When he started losing his temper with me, I concluded that there was something more involved than masculine temperament and I got nervous. There was something irrational about it on occasion."

"Did he become physically dangerous?" The words were almost formal in tone but that very formality told Abby just how intensely Torr was paying attention.

"There was only once," she whispered. "The last time I saw him..." She swallowed and focused very hard on the cars beside the river. "But up until then he seemed able to get control of himself before things got out of hand. I knew after a few weeks of seeing him, however, that I was going to have to get out of the relationship. I was beginning to feel trapped in a silk net. As long as I was sweet and agreeable and properly docile, Flynn played the role of Prince Charming. Whenever I strayed from my assigned role, he got increasingly unpleasant.

I knew it had been a mistake to get involved with him, but I didn't think it was too late to get out of the relationship without hard feelings. After all, he and I had never . . . I mean, it hadn't gotten to the point where we were . . ."

"You weren't sleeping together?"

"No. We weren't sleeping together." Torr had a way of cutting to the heart of the matter, Abby thought wryly. "At any rate, I told him I didn't intend to give up my other male friends, that I intended to keep dating other men. I implied I'd be seeing less of him."

"How did he take that?"

"He announced the next day that he and I were engaged," Abby said bluntly.

"Engaged!"

"I think he actually believed it. He had a way of convincing himself of anything he wanted to believe. As you can imagine, I was furious. I refused to see him again and made a point of dating other people. That's when I realized Flynn was potentially dangerous. He made wild accusations, called me unfaithful. When I pointed out that he had no claim on me, he went into a rage. It became uncomfortable to go into work. No one else in the office could figure out what was happening. If Flynn said we were engaged, they reasoned, then we must be engaged. Why would a high-ranking executive lie about a thing like that? When I denied it, everyone decided I must be playing hard to get. Flynn encouraged them to think I was just playing games. At work he was indulgent and charming toward me, as if he were humoring a recalcitrant female."

"What happened outside of work?"

"He began dropping by my apartment at odd hours, demanding to know who was in bed with me. When I told him the truth, that there was no one, he accused me of lying. He kept saying I was unfaithful, a cheat. Well, actually, he used somewhat more forceful language," Abby corrected unemotionally.

"So you finally quit your job?"

"In the end I made the mistake of going to his apartment one evening after he had made an ugly scene in front of a friend of mine, a man with whom I was having dinner. I told him to stop bothering me or I'd get some legal assistance. He lost control completely and struck me." Abby shivered, recalling that if she hadn't managed to escape through the door she'd left open, she would have found herself severely beaten, perhaps raped. She sensed the tension in Torr but her mind was turned inward, remembering the violence of that last scene. After a moment she continued. "I ran out of the apartment and into the street, found my car and drove back to a hotel. I was afraid to go home in case he followed me. The next morning at work he was back in his Prince Charming role, just as if nothing had happened. I realized no one would ever believe the way he had acted the night before. I quit that day and left town for a week to give myself some time to think. That was when I decided to start over in Portland."

"He didn't try to see you again?"

"No, thank heaven. He just disappeared from my life. Or I disappeared from his, depending on how you look at it," she tried to say flippantly. "And there you have it in a nutshell. That all happened two years ago and since then I've been very, very careful around men who have a tendency to become possessive."

"Not careful enough, apparently," Torr said coolly, rising to his feet and pulling her up beside him.

She frowned. "What's that supposed to mean?"

"You're involved with me and I'm going to be a very possessive lover, sweetheart." Torr lowered his head to kiss away the protest that came immediately to her lips, not releasing her until she relaxed against him. Finally he lifted his head and smiled down into her blue eyes. "But I won't rush you and I would never hurt you. When you finally trust me completely and understand my kind of possessiveness, I'll know that Randolph is really out of your life."

Abby tried to think of something else to say, some further explanation or protest, but nothing came to mind and she allowed herself to be led back toward the cabin. The questions and uncertainties hovered in her head until they reached the front door. Then Torr paused in the act of inserting the key into the lock.

"Well, well," he murmured, reaching down to pick up an envelope that had been half thrust under the doormat. "Looks like we missed someone interesting."

Abby shuddered, her eyes widening anxiously as she reached out to take the manila envelope from his hand.

"Do you want me to open it?" Torr asked softly, watching her with concern.

"No. I'll do it." She ripped at the tightly sealed envelope, her anger and fear making her movements impatient and erratic. The truth was, she hadn't wanted Torr to be the first to see whatever was inside. There might be more photos. How many more of those could Torr look at before he began to wonder if she'd told him the whole truth about that weekend?

With a final wrench she yanked open the envelope, spilling the contents awkwardly at her feet. Instantly she dropped down to collect the fallen papers. Torr knelt down beside her. He swore with soft savagery as his fingers closed around one of the items, a photocopy of a newspaper clipping, the kind made from files of newspapers kept on microfilm. Available in any public library.

"Abby, wait, let me get these," he ordered, but it was too late. She had already picked up another of the fallen clippings.

In stunned amazement she simply crouched there staring at the newspaper headline and the photo that accompanied it. The story carried a dateline from a midwestern city three years before.

The photo was of Torr Latimer and the headline announced that he was the brilliant corporate president whose wife had recently been found drowned under suspicious circumstances.

The smaller headline announced that there was speculation that Latimer had killed his wife in a jealous rage.

7

"OUR BLACKMAILER seems to do his homework fairly thoroughly." Torr ignored Abby's stunned expression, methodically picking up the scattered clippings and the note that accompanied them. He straightened and calmly finished unlocking the front door.

Abby, still crouching, stared after him for a timeless moment. He was acting as if nothing had happened. He was so monumentally cool about the whole thing while she was on the verge of exploding from a combination of fear and anger.

Speculation that Latimer had killed his wife in a jealous rage. Latimer, the brilliant successful head of a large corporation. Latimer, who had told her that he'd wanted a career change about three years before.

Latimer, whose amber eyes had flared with the promise of masculine possession, who'd claimed that Abby belonged to him now. Had his dead wife once seen that possessiveness? Been a victim of that claim?

Abby scrambled to her feet and followed Torr into the house. "The note," she managed in a voice that surprised her with its steadiness, "let me see the note that came with the clippings."

Torr carried the envelope and its contents into the kitchen and set them down on the table in a neat pile. The typed note was on top and he read it before silently handing it to Abby. She almost snatched it from his hand.

There is no safety with him. Latimer killed once because his woman was sleeping around. He'll do it again when he finds out what a little whore you are. You've jumped from the frying pan into the fire. Better run if you still can.

Shaking, Abby dropped into a chair beside the table. She stared sightlessly out the window, vaguely aware that Torr was preparing coffee. How could he do that, she wondered. How could he calmly make coffee while these clippings hung between them like a time bomb?

"I didn't kill her, you know," he said quietly as he waited for the coffee to filter into the pot. "The coroner's verdict was accidental drowning. She took the sailboat out by herself even though the weather reports had been bad. I wasn't home at the time. I was in New York on business."

Abby brought her gaze back to his as he set coffee down in front of her and took the seat on the other side of the table. "Was she . . . did she have another man?"

"Oh, yes, she had another man."

Abby stared at him, trying to read the stark shuttered expression in his eyes. "Did you know?"

"I knew."

"You quarreled?"

"We quarreled. Frequently."

"Why didn't you just get a divorce?" Abby asked painfully.

"I was going to file after I returned from New York."

"Why hadn't she filed already if she was in love with someone else?"

"She was more in love with her share of my income than she was with the other man. Money was always very important to Anne. She hadn't had a lot of it while she was growing up and the lack of it left its mark. She needed the financial security I could give her. But she didn't need me for much else."

There was no bitterness in his words. There was no emotion at all. Somehow that made Abby more nervous than anything else could have done. Torr's calm, cold response to her questions seemed unnatural. She reached across the table to where a row of her vitamin bottles had been neatly lined up. Selecting the vitamin B complex, she gulped down a couple, chasing them with the too-hot coffee.

"If your nerves are shaky, you probably shouldn't be drinking coffee," Torr observed mildly. "It would probably be more effective to stop the caffeine than to pop vitamin B."

"You're an expert on vitamin therapy now along with everything else?" She hadn't meant to snap at him like that. She wanted to stay in control of herself—as much in control as he was of himself. Hopeless task undoubtedly.

"I'm trying to become an expert on you. It's not easy." Torr's mouth relaxed briefly into a shadow of a smile. The expression hardened almost immediately when she didn't respond.

"Were you an expert on your wife?" Abby heard herself ask and was at once appalled at the question.

"I was at the end," he replied, shrugging. He stretched out his feet, examining the tips of his hand-sewn leather shoes. "This isn't getting us very far, is it? You look scared to death of me. But I'm not the one you're supposed to be frightened of, honey. It's the guy who sent the note and the clippings who should be giving you the case of nerves. I'm the one who's going to take care of you. Remember that."

Abby shook off the cobweb of conflicting emotions. She had to get control of herself and of the situation. She had to find out exactly what she was dealing with before she got any deeper into the mess. "Who are you, Torr? Who are you really? The man who was once head of this firm?" She indicated one of the clippings. "Or the man who trades commodities on his own?"

"I'm the man you met at a class in Japanese flower arrangement, Abby. No more, no less." He flicked a disparaging glance at the clipping that had his picture on it. "I haven't been him for nearly three years. I don't ever want to be him again. He had a job that demanded eighteen hours a day. He had a wife who couldn't be trusted. And in the end he had no friends. They all disappeared when the rumors started."

"The rumors?"

"The ones that suggested I might have killed Anne because she was unfaithful."

Abby caught her breath, alarmed at the queasiness in her stomach. "Why did they think you might have killed her?"

"Anne made a point of taking some of our quarrels public." The unpleasant look in Torr's eyes came and went. "She'd have too much to drink at a party and start telling everyone within earshot that I beat her, that she was an abused wife. On other occasions she'd hint to anyone who'd listen that I couldn't match her lover in the sack. During the last few months we rarely even saw each other. She was busy with her latest conquest and I was busy preparing for the divorce."

"You must have hated her at the end," Abby whispered.

"To tell you the truth, I don't know what I felt at the end. But I do know that she hated me. She disliked the fact that she was tied to me for financial reasons. Strongly resented that she needed me if she wanted to go on living the life-style she preferred. It infuriated her that I wouldn't tolerate her lovers. She claimed my jealousy was insane and that there were no grounds for it. The truth is that at the end I wasn't even jealous any longer. I just wanted out."

"You once told me that under certain circumstances any man could be made jealous and that any man might resort to violence."

"I didn't kill her, Abby." Torr gave her a steady glance.

Abby's eyes fell away, going back to the note and the clippings in front of her. "How did he know about . . . about all this?" she whispered. "The blackmailer . . ."

"An interesting question. One possibility is that he knew about the mess when it happened. As you can see, there was a lot of newspaper publicity. Most people would have forgotten but someone in the corporate world might have remembered because he would have known who I was at the time. Or the blackmailer might simply have done some investigation on his own. I doubt that, though. I think there's every possibility that the man we're looking for has some knowledge of the corporate world—enough to remember my name and a three-year-old scandal. When the payoff demands are finally made, I think we'll have a real handle on who we're dealing with."

Abby looked up questioningly. "What do you mean?"

"If the demands are for a small steady sum of cash, I think we can assume we're dealing with a petty crook. But if the blackmailer wants something else, something more sophisticated . . ." Torr broke off, rubbing his chin thoughtfully as his gaze went to the window.

"Like what, Torr?"

"We'll have to wait and see. It shouldn't be long. He wouldn't have gone to all this trouble if he weren't planning to act fairly soon. He's put the pressure on you and psychologically this would be the best time to make the payoff demands."

"Your knowledge of criminal psychology amazes me," she muttered.

"It's not a lot different from corporate psychology."

"That's a pretty cynical thing to say."

"And not particularly relevant," he agreed with a curious smile. "The real issue at hand now is what you're going to do, isn't it?"

Abby stiffened, folding her hands primly in front of her on the table and studying them as if they contained some answer she badly needed. "There's not much I can do until I hear what the blackmailer wants."

"You can run."

She looked sharply. "Is that what you think I'm going to do?" she whispered.

"I think the idea is flitting around in your head. Am I wrong?"

She moved uneasily and then got up to open the refrigerator door. Hunger was hardly a driving force at the moment, especially given the unstable condition of her stomach. But the need to do something active and seemingly purposeful was strong. Fixing lunch, while ridiculous on the surface, offered a much-needed physical goal. She ignored Torr's question, deliberately examining a plastic-wrapped brick of cheddar cheese.

"Am I wrong, Abby?" He didn't move from his chair but she could feel the intensity of his eyes on her back. "Are you thinking of running? Did the clippings achieve their objective?"

"What objective?" She located the lettuce.

"Obviously the blackmailer wants to scare you away from me. He doesn't want you under my protection. And he seemed to know just what string to pull to make you very nervous about my company, didn't he?" The last comment was rather thoughtful, as if Torr had just realized the full implications.

The words caught Abby's attention too, and she let the refrigerator door close slowly. "Yes. Yes, he did. You're right about one thing, Torr. Whoever is doing this seems to know me well."

Their eyes met across the room. "He not only knows about your protective feeling toward Cynthia, he also knows you're wary of men who have a reputation for dangerous jealousy and possessiveness."

How many people in the world knew her that well, Abby asked herself. It was terrifying to think that the blackmailer knew her so intimately. With a fierce scowl she began to make cheese sandwiches. The blackmailer was astute. Of all the strings he could have pulled to make her nervous about the dangers of staying with Torr Latimer, he'd found exactly the right one. She wondered what the arguments between Torr and his wife had been like. Violent? Cold and hostile? Torr was a strong man with a strong will. Crossing him would be dangerous under any circumstances, but even more so if he were crossed by a woman he considered his own. Abby shuddered as she sliced the bread, remembering the quiet resolute manner in which Torr had told her that she belonged to him. It was true he had put no pressure on her to return to his bed, but that didn't mean he wasn't feeling possessive. It only meant he was willing to be patient.

She was letting her imagination run away with her, Abby silently scolded herself. Just as the blackmailer would have wished. Savagely she slapped the sandwiches together, carried them over to the table and sat down. Torr didn't glance up. He was leafing through the pile of clippings.

"This envelope wasn't just meant for you," he remarked softly, drawing out another photo. "I think I was intended to see it, too."

"Another photo from that awful weekend?" Abby reached out to take it from his hand. Torr waited intently. "Oh, my God," she breathed. It was a picture of her again but the man with her wasn't Ward. It was a stranger. Someone she was certain she had never met.

And he was making obscene "love" to her on a sandy beach. The man's body covered hers and all that could be seen was her face.

Stricken, Abby let the photo drop from her hand as if it were on fire. It fell face down on the table and it was then that she saw the typed note on the back.

She's a whore, Latimer. She'll go to bed with anyone who has the cash. Just like your wife.

Abby's mouth went dry as Torr reached across to retrieve the photo. He flipped it back over, studying the scene. "Torr, I don't even know him. I swear, I've never been with that man. He's a total stranger. I...oh, I don't understand how . . ." She floundered to a halt, enraged and scared and helpless.

"A sandwich," he finally said, still staring at the photo.

"A sandwich! There are some right in front of you. What do you expect me to do—feed one to you?" It was a stupid thing over which to explode but Abby couldn't restrain herself. She sat glaring at him furiously as he glanced up from the photo. He looked first at her challenging expression and then at the pile of cheddar cheese sandwiches. Comprehension dawned.

"I didn't mean I wanted to eat one. I meant the photo is a sandwich. Your face, probably from one of the other shots, rephotographed with this woman's body and this man. A photographic sandwich. A little airbrushing would conceal the evidence of lines from the different photos."

Abby heard the explanation but her attention was suddenly on the whiteness around Torr's knuckles. She gazed in morbid fascination at the indication of his fury. Did he believe his own explanation? She licked her lips.

"You think someone deliberately made this photo to get at you?" she whispered. "To make you turn on me?"

"Who do you know who's into photography, Abby?"

"Oh, for pity's sake! Not more of your crazy detective work! I know a dozen people who are into photography. And who says it has to be someone who knows anything about photography? The blackmailer could have hired someone to do this . . . this sandwiching!"

"Maybe. Maybe not."

"How do you know it's a sandwich job?" Abby demanded rashly. "Maybe it really is me in the throes of passion with that . . . that person!"

He shook his head. "Not the throes of passion. I've seen what you look like in the throes of passion, remember? You don't gaze up at a man with a polite, serene little smile on your face as if you'd just been asked to tea."

Abby shot a suspicious glance at her tranquil, somewhat distant expression in the awful photograph. Hurriedly she glanced away. It made her almost physically ill to look at that picture and at the savage grip with which Torr held it. How did she look in the throes of passion, she wondered hysterically.

"Totally alive, vividly sensual, exciting, a little primitive. It's indescribable but it's definitely not serenely polite," Torr answered as if he'd just read her mind.

"Oh." She couldn't think of anything else to say. This man should know, she thought, exactly how she looked in bed. Anxiously she gnawed her lip. "Torr, I'm frightened."

"I know. It's working, isn't it?" He tossed down the picture and then collected the whole bunch of clippings and stuffed them back into the envelope.

"What is?"

"The blackmailer's plan to send you running out into the open like a startled rabbit. Out where you'll be easy to grab."

"I'm not running anywhere," she grumbled, irrationally glad now that the photo and the clippings were out of sight. She reached for a sandwich even though she wasn't in the least hungry. She decided to up her zinc intake too, and reached for the bottle of tablets.

"But you're thinking about it, aren't you?"

"I can hardly think straight at the moment!" Abby got up and stalked to the sink for a glass of water. But he was right, she silently admitted. She was thinking of running. Fear was a tangible sensation coiling around her, impeding her steps and clouding her mind.

The thick inhibiting stuff wasn't even focused on one particular aspect of the situation. By rights she should have been able to concentrate totally on the threat to herself from the blackmailer. Instead, other fears were hammering at her. There was a fear of having involved Torr in the mess. A fear of what he was thinking about her now that he'd seen those awful photos. A fear that he didn't believe her. A fear of what she would do if he decided the photos were real. It was all getting very complicated. She gulped the zinc tablets and stood staring at the faucet for a long moment.

From across the room Torr watched her narrowly. She looked ready to explode. High-strung, tense, nervous. About to run like a frightened creature.

He sat silent, trying to think of a way to stop her. She wasn't going to trust him completely—not now that she'd seen the newspaper clippings. Torr's hand curled into a large fist as he considered the prospect of getting hold of the blackmailer. Of all the times to have Abby find out about his past. She was beginning to accept and trust him, Torr thought. Just beginning to relax with him as a man. Now this. On the surface she might try very hard to believe his side of the story, but deep down could she fully relax around him again?

If she ran he might have trouble finding her. She could disappear for a matter of days or longer. By the time he caught up with her the blackmailer might already have found her. God only knew what would happen if that son of a bitch caught her first.

But how did you keep a woman from fleeing? Especially one who was clearly on the ragged edge of uncertainty and fear? If she trusted him completely, Torr decided, or at least knew for certain that she belonged to him, she might settle down and let him get on with the business of finding out who was behind the blackmail attempt. As it was he found himself fighting two battles—one for Abby's trust and one to track down her tormentor.

The unstable situation festered between them for the rest of the afternoon. Torr was careful to lock the photos and clippings out of sight but they obviously were not out of mind, not for Abby. She made a pretense of reading several magazines that she had bought at the village store. Then she silently tried to work on a crossword puzzle, not asking Torr for any help. He watched her drink a half dozen cups of coffee and wondered if all the vitamins she took every couple of hours could counter the caffeine.

How much longer before she tried to leave? he asked himself. Would she simply announce she wanted to be taken home to Portland? Or would she grab the keys tonight and sneak off on her own?

Talk about having one's nerves on edge, Torr decided grimly. His own were rapidly approaching a flash point. He couldn't think of anything brilliantly reassuring or humorous or thought-provoking to say. The silence between himself and Abby grew. With every passing hour it seemed heavier and more impossible to breach.

Should he tell her more about his doomed marriage? he wondered. No, it seemed best to let that topic lapse. There was nothing much to say, when you got right down to it. It had been a disaster from start to finish. If he went into further gruesome detail, Abby might begin to wonder if there was more to the story than he had admitted.

If he told her about the frustration and the anger and the embarrassment he had endured during the short term of his marriage, Abby might believe that he was building a justification that was not really necessary if he were truly innocent of murder.

No, scratch that topic. Maybe he should try involving her once again in some detective work. After all, they ought to be studying the list of people she knew in light of all the information they now had. But Abby didn't look as if she were interested in going over that list again.

Somehow they were missing something, though. Torr was sure of it. Blackmail was a rather intimate crime. It required the perpetrator not only have highly confidential information, but know just how damaging that information could be. It required a kind of intimacy that could not be ignored. Whoever was threatening Abby was not merely some creep on the street who'd happened to snap a few photos by accident.

All during the silent dinner that he had prepared, Torr's thoughts kept ricocheting back and forth between the possible identity of the blackmailer and the very urgent problem of how to deal with Abby's increasing withdrawal.

It wasn't until they were silently sipping cognac in front of the fire that Torr decided there were priorities that had to be set. He was going to go out of his mind if he didn't establish the bonds between himself and Abby once and for all.

He glanced at her from beneath half-lowered lashes, noticing the flush on her cheek as she stared fixedly into the crackling flames. She was a million miles away, he surmised. Probably planning her escape. He would wake up in the morning and find her gone.

Torr realized with a sudden wrenching sensation in his gut that he couldn't allow that to happen. She was his now, whether she knew it or not. In that moment he could think of no other way to enforce the knowledge on her than by the most fundamental of methods.

The only way to make certain Abby was still with him in the morning was to take her to bed tonight and keep her there. It might not say a lot for his intelligence that he'd been driven to such an extreme conclusion, but he knew it was the truth.

Legs apart, Torr leaned forward and carefully set the cognac glass down on the coffee table in front of him. He concentrated intently on the amber liquid in the glass as he spoke.

"How are you going to do it, Abby? Will you try to steal the keys in the middle of the night or will you go upstairs, pack and then demand to be driven back to Portland?"

Her head swung around and he read the guilty amazement in her eyes. Torr felt himself tighten as he realized he'd come very close to guessing her thoughts. Didn't she understand? He couldn't allow her to leave. Not now. Not after what they had shared.

"I might as well tell you that I won't drive you back to Portland. So I think we're left with the possibility of key theft," he mused, his eyes focusing on the fire. He could feel the tension in her as she sat at the far end of the sofa, staring at his profile. He was probably scaring her but it couldn't be helped. He was extremely scared himself.

"What are you talking about?" she demanded stiffly. "I have no intention of stealing the car keys."

"No? Then how did you plan on running tonight, Abby?"

"Who said anything about running?"

"It's been written all over your face since that envelope arrived. Do you think I can't read your eyes? Don't you think I can see the fear in them?"

"It seems to me that I have a right to be afraid," she protested.

"Perhaps. But not of me."

She surged to her feet. "Doesn't it occur to you that I might be afraid *for* you rather than *of* you?" She wasn't looking at him, however, when she spoke, and Torr guessed that she didn't want him to see her expression.

"There's no reason to be afraid for me. I've told you I'm in this with you by choice. Don't use that as an excuse, Abby."

"I'm not making excuses!" She whirled, confronting him, her head high, her body rigid with tension. "This is my problem, Torr. I had no right to get you involved. It's very nice of you to want to help, but I—"

"Very nice of me!" The words came from him in a soft explosion as he leapt off the sofa in a smooth, taut movement. "Abby, the last thing I feel toward you is *nice*. I have never felt any inclination to be *nice* to you. Lady, I want to take you to bed. I want to protect you. I want you to know in the very depths of your soul that you belong to me, but none of that has anything to do with being *nice!*"

She flinched as he challenged her, automatically taking a step backward. There was no farther room for retreat, Torr saw. The fire crackled directly behind her. He suddenly realized he was scaring the daylights out of her. Smoky blue eyes flared at him with desperate

determination. Her soft body was held unnaturally
still, poised to flee or fight. He'd handled this all wrong.
He shouldn't have pushed her like this. But what else
could he have done? His own raging uncertainty was
eating at him, forcing him to take some definitive action.

"Don't threaten me, Torr!"

"I'm not threatening you." But he was and they both
knew it.

"I don't need anyone else trying to push me around
at this particular moment in my life. I thought you were
being kind and...and considerate. You were willing to
wait and let our relationship evolve naturally. It ap-
pears instead that all this week you've been leading me
on, making me think you understood my feelings. But
maybe that's because you thought I was a different kind
of woman. Maybe you have behaved nicely because
you thought I was a nice woman. Now you've seen all
the photos, haven't you? Now you know that my one
weekend at the beach with Ward wasn't just a fluke or
a set of circumstances that someone twisted to his own
advantage. Oh, no. Now you've seen evidence that I do
that sort of thing a lot. What was it the note said? I'll
sleep with anyone for the right amount of cash. A
whore. How that must grate on you, Torr. How could
you be so unlucky as to get involved with another female like your first wife?"

"Abby, shut up! You don't know what you're saying."

"Of course I know what I'm saying. Don't you think
I saw the way your fingers were clenched around that
photograph of me and that other man? You were utter-

ing all the nice reassuring things, but you were thinking something entirely different. You were wondering about me, weren't you, Torr? Wondering if I was going to be just like your wife. Well, you don't have to worry about it. I'm not about to get any more involved with you. For both our sakes it's best if I get out of here. Now. Tonight."

"You're not going anywhere." Torr could hear the deadly certainty in his own words, and the effect on Abby was instantaneous. She moved, circling to the right since there was no farther room to retreat. As if he were a wolf, she tried to put distance between them without making any sudden moves that might set off his primitive attack instincts.

"I have to leave, Torr. I've been thinking about it all afternoon."

"Don't you think I realize that? I've been watching you drift further and further away from me ever since that blasted envelope arrived. But I'm not going to let you leave, Abby. There's no way you can walk back to Portland and you'll have to get past me to get the keys."

"Why, Torr?" she got out starkly. "Why are you doing this? Because you can't bear the thought that you've gotten mixed up with another unreliable, untrustworthy female? Do you have to prove something to yourself?"

"Maybe. Most of all I have to prove something to you."

"Don't threaten me, Torr!"

"Stop fighting me," he countered, revolving slowly to follow her wary circling movement. "Abby, be rea-

Uneasy Alliance

sonable. There's nowhere to run tonight. Stay here with me where you're safe. Trust me, honey."

"Do you trust me?" she whispered tightly.

"Yes."

"I don't believe you! I saw the way you looked at that photograph," she wailed. "You looked as though you wanted to kill someone."

"Not you!" he rasped. "Abby, honey, not you. Surely you realize that?"

"Do I?"

Torr tried to steady his flaring instincts with a measure of self-control. It was almost impossible. She was going to run. He had been right. Look at her, trying to circle toward the door so that she could flee out into the night. What did she hope to accomplish by that?

"Abby, panic isn't going to solve anything."

"I'm leaving, Torr."

"No."

"You can't stop me."

He smiled crookedly, almost gently. "Can't I?"

The implied threat was enough to break her last shreds of control, just as he had known it would be. There was no sense putting off the inevitable. She might as well make the break that would bring about the final result.

"Damn you, Torr!"

She swung around and threw herself past him. Torr caught her easily, his large hands closing inexorably around her waist, dragging her back against his body. She fought with a wiry, feminine strength he hadn't expected her to possess. In his grasp Abby twisted and writhed, her desperation plain in her silence. She wasn't wasting any energy in screaming at him. Every ounce of it was being spent on the battle.

She didn't stand a chance, of course. She was ultimately too soft and too small to defeat him. Torr simply held her wrapped to the length of him, avoiding her kicking feet while he kept her arms still by pinning them to her sides.

"Abby, honey, stop it. There's no need—"

She interrupted his words by jerking herself fiercely to the right. Torr let the momentum carry them both down, guiding the fall so that they landed in a tangled heap on the sofa. At the last instant he twisted slightly so that he came down on top of her and after that there was no way for Abby to continue the battle. She was immobilized on her stomach beneath his superior weight.

"Abby. Abby, sweetheart, don't cry." Alarmed at the little gasping sounds she was making beneath him, Torr raised himself slightly away from her body.

"I'm not crying. I'm trying to breathe. You weigh a ton!"

"Sorry, darling." He continued to hold himself partially away from her, his hand automatically beginning to stroke her back down to the full curve of her hip. "Take it easy. I won't hurt you. I swear I won't hurt you."

Still trapped by his sprawling leg and the firm grip of his hand, Abby sniffed back the sobs of frustration and anger. She would *not* allow herself to cry.

"Torr, you have no right to treat me like this. You can't keep me here against my will."

"I can't let you go," he retorted simply.

His hand continued to move on her back, gentling her until she wanted to cry out again in protest. He had no right to have such an effect on her. She should be running for her life. What did she really know about this man? He could be far more dangerous than Flynn Randolph had been. After all, the clippings said people had thought him capable of killing his wife in a jealous rage.

Burying her face in the cushion she inhaled huge, muffled breaths. The big hand on her body was working a heavy magic, and in silence captive and captor considered their options.

From Abby's point of view those options were remarkably limited.

She felt totally enveloped by the heat and weight of Torr's body. Even though he had lifted himself partially off her there was no way she could have moved. His thigh lay over the back of her legs. With one arm wrapped under her breast he held her pinned close to his muscular length and he let her feel just enough of his waiting strength to know that she was completely outgunned and outmaneuvered. By all rights she ought to be in a raging panic.

"Torr?"

"Hmmm?" He continued to caress her, his hand moving down over her tightly jeaned thigh.

"Are you . . . are you going to force me?"

There was a fractional silence. Then: "Would it be necessary?"

It was her turn for silence. From out of nowhere her spirit flared to counter the masculine intent she heard in his tone. "If you think I'm just going to lie here meekly and let you control me with sex, you're out of your mind!"

The gentling hand stopped on the high, firm curve of her buttock. Abby felt his fingers clench powerfully and she knew a spasm of excitement. Memories of his previous lovemaking flooded her body. Memories of his determined concern for her safety flooded her mind. All in all she felt totally inundated by Torr Latimer.

Slowly he shifted her around until she lay on her back. "Nobody could control you with sex, Abby," Torr said softly, amber eyes reflecting the flickering light of the fire. "But I think, just possibly, a man could control you with love."

As his mouth came down on hers, Abby felt a spiraling tension that combined with Torr's touch to leave her lying helpless beneath him. *Oh God,* she thought on a stricken note. *He knows. He knows I've fallen in love with him.*

8

WITH LOVE CAME TRUST. Or maybe it was the other way around. In a distant corner of her mind, Abby wondered which had come first for her. Perhaps they had both arrived together in an inseparable knot that now chained her to Torr Latimer.

But it was impossible to think logically at the moment. Torr's mouth covered hers with consuming power, leaving her no option but to respond. As always when he held her, Abby wanted only to succumb completely to the intoxicating warmth of their lovemaking. She felt his hands on her body, aware that he was loosening her clothing, and her determination to flee disintegrated.

Torr felt her enthralling surrender as he steadily unbuttoned the muted plaid shirt she wore. The softness in her seemed to flow and strain beneath his hands, inviting and challenging and captivating. He had been right, he decided exultantly. Right to force the issue tonight. Right to take her into his arms and show her that neither of them could flee from the magic that flared between them.

"I shouldn't have given you so much time this past week," he murmured as he parted the edges of her shirt and slid his hand inside to find her breasts. "I should have just taken you to bed again and again until you realized how much I need you. Abby, I've tried to teach you to trust me. Tried to do things your way and still protect you. But tonight you were going to run and I couldn't let you do that."

"I thought..." Abby broke off, a soft cry of rising need in her throat. "I thought it would be for the best. Torr, please believe me. I never should have let you get involved."

He growled his displeasure as he leaned over to force the words back into her mouth with his tongue. Hadn't he told her often enough that she'd had no choice when it came to his involvement? With hunger and a desire to silence her protests, Torr explored the dark territory behind her lips. The taste of her there fed his appetite, making him ravenous for the other delicious parts of her.

Beneath his palm he could feel the budding nipple and he vaguely heard his own husky groan of response. She came alive for him in a way that no other woman ever had. Or was it that he came alive for her? With Abby, Torr knew the full measure of himself as a man. The experience was primitive, almost savage in some respects. Perhaps she had been right to fear the possessiveness in him, he acknowledged silently. How could he explain he'd never been totally aware of it himself until he'd met her? He only knew now that he could never let her go.

The warmth of the firelight bathed Abby's skin in gold as Torr pushed back her shirt, baring her breasts completely.

"Abby, honey. You're so soft, so wonderfully soft. How did you ever think I could let you go? I need your softness, sweetheart. I need it more than I've ever needed anything else in my life."

She twined her arms around his neck, offering her throat as her head fell back over his arm. Torr found the hollow where her pulse thrummed and kissed it. She moaned, lifting herself against him and he thought he would go out of his mind.

"Torr, my darling. You make me feel so wild," she breathed against his neck.

He caught her hand and put her fingers on the first button of his shirt. She needed no further urging. As she fumbled to open the garment, Torr found the fastening of her jeans. When he unzipped the denims he was unable to resist plunging his hand down into the moist warmth of her, and when he found it, he knew that he could not be the gallant patient lover he had been last time.

"Abby, honey, I'm going to take you tonight. Make you mine. Do you understand? Afterward you won't have any more doubts. You won't be able to run. I'll have you chained too close to my heart."

She stirred against him as he stripped the jeans down her legs and let them drop to the floor. Her body seemed to be a sensuous trap of golden skin and shadowy heat. It was a trap he longed to spring.

Torr leaned over her, letting his chest crush her breasts as he yanked off his trousers. The hardness of her nipples made him catch his breath and then he was naked beside her. Deliberately he let her feel the waiting fullness of his manhood, testing himself against her thigh.

"When I take you it's like diving into the softest, deepest petals of a flower," he rasped. "I don't know how I've been able to wait so long. And I know I can't wait any longer."

"No," she whispered throatily, denying him nothing. "Neither can I."

He slipped his hand between her thighs, glorying in the silken skin there. Then he was pushing apart her legs, lifting himself to angle her beneath him. She moved obediently to his touch, wrapping him close as he sank down onto her.

When he felt the heated dampness of her body waiting to sheath him, Torr drove into her with a husky groan. He had to take his fill of her or lose his mind. She clung to him, her legs tangling with his, her nails leaving small savage marks in his back.

She wanted him, needed him, he told himself exultantly. No woman could fake this kind of soft, clinging need. And even if it were possible, Abby would disdain such faked passion. For her everything had to be real. She was too vibrant and excitingly alive to play sophisticated games in bed. Knowing that was what gave him hope and roused a fierce determination in him. He would make love to her until she could do nothing but cry out her need of him, and once he had the words he would never let her forget them.

"Tell me," he half snarled against the skin of her breast. "Tell me you want me. Tell me what it's like for you." With controlled, passionate violence he raided her body, unlocking the treasure of crushed petals waiting there. Plunging into them again and again with unpredictable strokes that elicited the soft cries at the back of her throat. Cries he loved to swallow.

"Torr, Torr. I want you. I've never wanted any man the way I want you. Oh, Torr!"

He felt the passionate spasm that coursed through her, tightening her body around his until he was as caught up in the climax as she was. It pulled at him, seeking to drain him. Torr could no more resist the primitive tide than he could have ignored the pull of ocean waves. With a muffled shout of satisfaction he gave himself up to the endless sea of velvet petals, aware that Abby was already drifting blissfully in his arms.

Torr was not going to allow her to drift all the way into sleep, Abby realized vaguely as his tongue flickered over the film of perspiration on her breasts. She came drowsily back to the surface, lifting her lashes to meet his gaze. There was satisfaction in his amber eyes, satisfaction and a challenging question. As she looked up at him he touched her faintly bruised mouth with the tip of one blunt finger.

"You want me, Abby."

"Yes." There didn't seem much point in denying that now.

"You need me."

"Yes."

"I can feel all that when you're here in my arms. You couldn't lie with your body. It isn't possible for you."

"You sound very sure of that."

He moved in the equivalent of a massive shrug. Nothing could have made his agreement more obvious. Abby was torn between a purely feminine desire to slap him for his masculine arrogance and an equally feminine desire to submit to it. He must have read the conflicting thoughts in her eyes because his look softened abruptly and he dipped his head to brush a small kiss against the tip of her nose.

"Don't be angry. I can't help the truth. It exists for both of us. I needed to have you admit it, though, because I think only when you've admitted it aloud will you accept it. And when you've accepted it you can trust me. Really trust me."

"That's important to you?"

"It's vital to me, honey. I nearly went crazy this afternoon watching and waiting for you to get the nerve to run."

"I wasn't going to run," she protested quickly.

"Yes, you were."

"I only thought it best to get away. I don't want you hurt by all this, Torr."

"The only way I can be hurt is if you don't trust me enough to let me help you."

She inhaled deeply, aware of the scent of his damp musky body and of the fragrance of the log fire. She was still lying trapped beneath Torr, her limbs snarled with his. His weight crushed her into the sofa and he made no move to release her.

"I don't want to hurt you, Torr."

"Then you'll have to trust me."

Abby searched his face anxiously. "What about you? Do you trust me? I saw the way you looked at that photo. I know what you must have been thinking...."

"I was thinking that I would like to get my hands on the man who's blackmailing you. And I'll admit that the thoughts were a little violent. But the violence wasn't aimed at you, sweetheart. That's what you have to bring yourself to believe. Trust me, Abby. Please trust me."

"I do," she whispered huskily. "I do."

He sighed and lowered his head to her breast. "I didn't kill her, Abby."

"I know that."

"And I would never hurt you."

"I know that, too. I've known it all along, I suppose."

"I kept dreading the day you found out about my past," he admitted. "I was afraid you'd only compare me with that man who once frightened you."

Abby shook her head. "You're nothing like Flynn Randolph."

"How am I different?" he demanded, letting his fingers trail tantalizingly down her waist to her hip and back.

"A million ways," she replied, smiling above his head. Men. They asked far more personal questions than did women. The firelight flickered on Torr's black hair and it made her smile broaden. "For one thing your hair is a different color. His was brown."

"That's an enormous difference, all right," he complained. "Can't you do any better than that?"

"Well, let's see. You're built a lot differently than he was. You're sort of like a rock. He was tennis-player thin."

"Abby, I'm warning you...."

"I'm trying to reassure you," she protested. "Let me see, what else is different about you? I certainly would never have met him in a class on the art of Japanese flower arrangement. He was into other kinds of hobbies."

"Something nice and macho like race-car driving?" Torr sounded as though he might be growing annoyed. The little game wasn't going the way he wanted it to go.

"No, as a matter of fact, he was into—" Abby shut her mouth with a snap as the memory flashed into her mind. An image of Flynn with his camera, irritated with her because she would not pose in the nude for him. Another image of him in his elaborately equipped darkroom. "Photography," Abby finally got out unemotionally. "Flynn was into photography."

Torr was suddenly very still and tense. There was a dangerous silence while they both absorbed what she had just said, and then he sat up slowly.

"Brown hair, you said?"

Abby licked her lips. "Yes."

"Thin?"

"Yes, oh Torr, surely—"

"And he's into photography?"

"Well, he was when I knew him, but that was two years ago. Why would he . . . ? It makes no sense, Torr. Why would he do something like this? After two years?"

"He knows how you feel about Cynthia?" Torr kept up the questions, pushing himself away from her. He stood up, stalking restlessly over to stand gazing down into the fire.

Abby watched him, acutely aware of the hard muscled maleness of him as he stood in the glow of the flaring firelight. So strong, so thoroughly masculine. She could still feel the heavy imprint of his body on hers.

"He knew," Abby admitted slowly, frowning intently. "But, Torr, it doesn't make any sense. It was all over between Flynn and myself two years ago. He was glad to see the last of me. Claimed he never wanted to see me again. Called me a...a..." Her voice trailed off as she remembered the note on the back of the ugly photograph they had received that morning. "Called me a whore."

"Hell." Torr ran his fingers through his black and silver hair. "Abby, he's not on our list." He swung around, amber eyes shadowed and hawklike. *"Why on earth wasn't he on that list?"*

Abby flinched from the fierce demand in his voice, coiling her legs under her and reaching instinctively for her shirt. "Torr, listen to me. There's no way Flynn could be the blackmailer. It's been two whole years since I saw him. Why on earth would he pop up now to cause trouble?"

"I want to know why he's not on that list I had you put together. He's got brown hair, he's into photography, he knows all your vulnerable points. Lady, did you think I was playing games with that blasted list? I wanted everyone on it who fit the profile. Everyone. Not just your present friends and associates!"

Abby slipped on her shirt and pulled it around her in a tense, protective motion. Her eyes were wide and wary now as she watched the man who only moments before had been making passionate love to her. This was a side of Torr she had never seen before and it was a revelation. From out of nowhere she recalled the newspaper clippings that had described him as a powerful, ruthlessly successful corporate president.

Torr might be standing naked in front of a cozy fire but she didn't need much imagination to picture him dressed in a sleek gray suit and bearing the natural authority of a corporate shark. There was a controlled power in the man that was independent of time, place or clothing.

It also didn't take much imagination to visualize herself in the role of a subordinate who had badly fouled up an important assignment. Resentfully Abby stirred on the couch, darting a glance at her jeans and wondering if she could pull them on from where she sat.

"There's no need to yell at me, Torr."

"I am not yelling at you," he bit out roughly, "but if you want to know the truth, I'm seriously considering doing a lot more than that. Right now I could cheerfully take my belt to that sweet backside of yours. Thanks to your idiotic refusal to follow orders, we've overlooked one of the prime suspects. A man who may very well be a little sick in the head from the way you've described him. A man who fits the profile. How many other possible candidates have you left off the list?"

"None! I haven't left anyone else off except . . . except—" her voice lowered and became almost inaudible "—maybe a couple of people who couldn't possibly have . . ."

"Such as?" Torr demanded.

Abby glared at him, her mouth tight with resentment. He was standing with his feet braced slightly apart, his hands fitted to his hips. The controlled aggression in him was so strong she half expected to see it manifest itself in some visible form.

"Torr, if you start listing every possible candidate, there'd be no stopping. Good grief! How many brown-haired men do you think I've met in my life?"

"I have no idea. I've asked you to tell me. On several occasions."

"Look, if I started doing that I'd have to include people like Ward!"

"Tyson? Your cousin's husband? He's got brown hair?"

"Well, yes, but—"

"He's into photography?"

"Judging from the number of photos of the baby I get every couple of weeks, I suppose you could say that," Abby shot back caustically. "Torr, every new father is into photography."

"Who else?" He ignored her angry response.

"I don't know! I can't think of anyone else. Torr, you're acting as though you're conducting an inquisition!"

"You're right," he muttered, gliding forward until he was only inches away from the couch, scowling down at her. "What's more, you're going to submit to it. If you'd done things right the first time instead of in your usual haphazard undisciplined style, we wouldn't be going through this tonight. I was a fool to go so easy on you. I should have known that unless I pushed, you wouldn't really give your full attention to that list. From the beginning I've been far too cautious with you."

"I'm not one of your employees!"

He reached down, his large hands closing around her upper arms. As if she were light as a feather, he lifted her a few inches off the floor, holding her so that she was eye to eye with him. "You can say that again," Torr admonished. "You're not an employee. You're my woman. It is my responsibility to protect you. You will obey clear and reasonable orders from me when your safety is involved. Is that simple enough for you? Do you understand exactly what I'm saying?"

Abby blinked, helpless in his iron grasp, feeling idiotically vulnerable in her near-nakedness. Somehow Torr didn't seem at all vulnerable in his lack of clothing. Sheer masculine dominance was more than adequate to cloak him. She swallowed and then said in a very low voice, "I understand."

"Excellent," he replied silkily. He lowered her so that her feet found the floor, then continued to lean intimidatingly over her. "Look at me, Abby." Gnawing her lip warily, she obeyed. "We've played this waiting game long enough. Tomorrow we act. We've got enough leads to pursue now. Too many to justify sitting here like a couple of clay pigeons. In the morning we'll head for Seattle. I want to talk to Tyson."

"Ward? But, Torr, I didn't want to bring him into this."

"He's already into it. I should have tackled him in the beginning," Torr muttered in disgust. "Instead I let myself be persuaded to go along with your plans."

"But Ward can't be the blackmailer! It makes no sense!"

"I didn't say he was. But he's part of this mess one way or another and it's time we informed him of that fact."

"I don't want to handle it that way."

"What you want is not particularly important to me at the moment, Abby. Getting you out of this crazy situation is all that matters right now. Go upstairs and climb into bed. It's late and we'll be leaving here first thing in the morning. I'll take care of the fire."

He turned away without waiting for her response and began settling the remains of the flickering logs with a set of brass tongs. Torr heard Abby move around behind him, silently collecting her clothing and starting across the floor to the staircase. His hand tightened on the cold brass in his grip as he waited to see which room she would go to when she reached the top of the stairs.

He'd been a little rough on her, he acknowledged grimly. But he'd had no choice. What had she expected him to do when he realized how severely she had hampered the investigation by not cooperating fully when he had asked for names for the list? Of course she hadn't intentionally refused to cooperate. It was simply that she was used to doing things her own way—haphazardly, without discipline.

While he approached everything in a far more thorough fashion.

She was at the top of the stairs now. He could barely hear the pad of her feet on the hardwood floor. She hadn't said a word when he'd ordered her up to bed. Just turned and climbed the stairs.

He shouldn't have chewed her out like that, he told himself. She was probably furious. Her anger he could handle. It was having her afraid of him that worried him. Had he frightened her with his tirade? Undone all the progress he'd made this past week?

The questions ravaged him as he hung up the tongs and pulled the screen shut in front of the hot coals. She'd deserved the tongue-lashing. As he'd told her, she was lucky that was all it amounted to tonight. If she was going to run upstairs and cower in her own room he would just have to follow her inside and yank her back out. From now on she belonged in his bed and it was time she knew it. Matters were too serious at the moment to allow her the luxury of taking her time.

The scrape of the screen in front of the fire hid the last of Abby's footsteps. When Torr straightened and started for the stairs all was silent on the floor above. Which bedroom had she entered? he wondered.

He stalked up the stairs two at a time, aware of a pounding in his veins that was composed of equal parts of desire, irritation and fear. Fear that everything he'd managed to accomplish this past week had come apart in his hands because of those newspaper clippings and because he'd reached the end of his patience.

Which bedroom?

He strode past his own room, which was still dark, and came to a halt in front of the closed door of the room Abby had been using. He would be kind but firm. No, he would be polite and as gallant as possible. He'd try to repair a few of the fences he'd just ripped apart. He'd try to talk to her, apologize but explain that he hadn't any real choice. There were things that had to be done.

Hell, he'd simply go in there and pull her out of bed, toss her over his shoulder and carry her back to his room. One way or another she was going to learn something important tonight.

Half expecting to find the door locked, Torr wrenched the handle. It opened easily and he found himself gazing through the shadows into a still-made bed.

Anticipation and an incredible relief sizzled in him. She hadn't crept back to the safety of her own room! Spinning around he paced back down the hall to his bedroom. Pushing open the door he stepped inside, letting his eyes adjust to the darkness.

It wasn't hard to pick out Abby's gentle curves under the quilt.

"You lied to me," she murmured.

"No." His protest was soft, almost anguished. He couldn't move.

"Yes, you did." She held a corner of the quilt back, silently inviting him into the bed. "You said you never pounce."

Torr closed his eyes briefly in rueful relief and then opened them and started forward. "Do you feel pounced upon?"

"Very. Physically and verbally." But her eyes were gleaming and Torr groaned heavily as he lay down beside her.

"How was I to know you would bring out the beast in me?"

"I think it came out naturally."

Torr's mouth moved over hers before she could say anything else. This time, he promised himself, he would take it slow, warm her with care and attention to detail until she cried out for more. He wanted to hear his name on her lips over and over again. He'd never get his fill of that soft demand.

THE NEXT MORNING Abby grumblingly accepted Torr's decision on the subject of confronting Ward Tyson. She did not do so without protest, however. Torr endured the complaints, arguments, reasoned logic and infuriated pleas with stoic patience all during breakfast, the packing of the car and the drive back toward Portland and then north to Seattle. It was a long trip, several hours in fact, and Abby tried not to waste a minute of the time.

"I see no reason to involve Ward at this point. He can't do anything and he might feel that he has to tell Cynthia the truth about that weekend in order to get me off the hook," she began.

"He might," Torr agreed.

"Well, I don't want Cynthia told. That's the whole object of this exercise!"

"Certainly the blackmailer's logic."

"Torr, I'm talking about a lifetime relationship with my cousin which will be ruined by all this."

"Just remember that you didn't ruin it. Tyson did."

"Ruining that marriage will be an even more damaging act," she argued. "I don't see why we have to do anything at this point. Give it a little more time."

"Time only serves on the blackmailer's side. It gives him an opportunity to work on your nerves, wear you down and wear you out. Tyson is not the only man we're going to see. As soon as an actual extortion attempt is made, we're going to call in the police. I'd do it now except for the fact that all we have are pictures and implied threats."

Abby stared at him. "You seemed like such a nice man when I first met you!"

"What am I now?"

"Domineering, arrogant and overbearing," she declared with a certain malicious satisfaction. "You've taken over my life and it worries me because I don't know how to stop you or control you."

"When this is all over I promise you will find me easy enough to manage again." The assurance was gently given and Abby didn't trust it for an instant.

"Will you listen to me while I try to explain why I don't want to contact Ward at this point," she muttered, folding her arms across her breasts while she sat stiffly in the car seat.

"I don't have much of a choice except to listen, do I? It's a small car."

"But you're not going to pay any attention, right?"

"We're going to talk to Tyson, honey," he said with great finality.

Abby dreaded the meeting for the entire length of the drive. Several hours later as Torr followed her directions off Interstate 5 into downtown Seattle, she was wildly considering leading him on a goose chase through the high-rise office buildings. But something about the grim manner in which he drove convinced her that might not be the wisest move. With a sigh she guided him to the underground parking lot of the building that housed the headquarters of Lyndon Technologies.

She had expected anything from astonishment to shock on Ward's handsome face when his secretary showed them into his office. But she couldn't possibly have anticipated his half-furious, half-relieved greeting.

"Where on earth have you been, Abby? I've been trying to get hold of you for nearly a week!" He shot up from behind his desk, every inch the executive in his dark suit and crisp white shirt. "Sit down. I've got to talk to you. Something important has come up. Who's this?" He swung a challenging, assessing glance at the silent man who stood by Abby's side.

"The man who's claiming exclusive rights for the privilege of yelling at Abby," Torr said, with an unmistakable chill in his voice. "So I'd appreciate it if you would apologize to her and refrain from using that tone with her in the future. My name's Torr Latimer." He didn't extend his hand. Instead he made a point of politely seating Abby and then taking the leather chair next to hers.

Abby winced at the casual aggression in his words. Lately it was becoming very easy to visualize Torr in his previous role of corporate head. Ward stared at the stranger, a calculating respect in his eyes telling Abby more than words could have exactly how Torr was measuring up in the other man's estimation. One dark-brown brow arched as he inclined his head with mocking formality.

"My apologies, Abby. Where'd you meet the knight in shining armor?"

"At a class in flower arranging," Abby retorted. "Ward, something serious has happened. Torr insists you should be involved. I didn't want to come here today, but—"

"But I overrode her objections," Torr interrupted.

"I see." Ward sat down in his swivel chair and regarded the other two across the expanse of his desk.

"Well, it would seem as though we've all got news. Suppose you go first."

Abby frowned. She knew Ward well enough to read the genuine concern in his hazel eyes. "It's not Cynthia or the baby, is it? Are they all right?"

Ward shook his head abruptly. "They're fine. My problem is a business one. What's yours?"

"Hers is business of a sort, also. Blackmail." Torr let the shock of his words sink in and then went on bluntly. "It concerns you too, that's why we're here."

"Blackmail!" Ward looked stunned. "Is this a joke?"

"Unfortunately, no," Abby answered, sighing. She glanced hastily at Torr and realized from the set expression on his face that he wasn't going to let her find a way around the issue. "Remember . . . remember that weekend at the coast, Ward?"

"Oh, not that." Wearily Ward rubbed his thumb and forefinger along the bridge of his nose, eyes closing for a long moment. "What is going on, Abby?"

"Someone took some pictures. Photos of us . . . you and me coming out of a hotel room." Abby felt a flush rise into her face as she tried to explain the awkward situation.

"Pictures!" Ward's eyes snapped open, zeroing in on Torr, not Abby. "Incriminating photos?"

"They could be. To Cynthia." Bleakness underlined Abby's words. "I'm sorry, Ward. I didn't know what to do. Torr saw the pictures and figured out what was going on. He insisted on confronting you. He says you're involved."

"Well, I was, wasn't I?" Ward gave her a laconic glance before returning his concentration on Torr. "How much do you know, Latimer?"

"Everything."

"Wrung the whole sordid tale out of Abby here, huh?"

"It wasn't easy."

"I'll bet it wasn't. She's an independent woman with a mind of her own."

"But inclined to be a bit impulsive in her behavior," Torr observed gently. "She wanted to handle the whole mess all by herself."

"She would," Ward growled. "Well, what happened? Threats? Payoff demands?"

"No demands, not yet at any rate. Soon, I expect," Torr said, his eyes cool and unreadable. "I knew you wouldn't want Abby facing an extortionist all by herself."

"Whoever it is has threatened to tell Cynthia about our, uh, illicit weekend, is that it?" Ward gazed thoughtfully at Abby, who shifted uncomfortably, her heart going out in sympathy for him.

"I'm afraid so."

"Interesting," Ward mused. "Who knows you well enough to realize that's a valid threat?"

"That was one of Torr's first questions," Abby grumbled, aware that the two men were a well-matched pair. Both of them thought along the same lines and with the same straight-to-the-point logic.

"Any answers?" Ward swung back to Torr.

"A few possibilities." Torr looked at him.

"Fascinating," Ward remarked dryly.

"Fascinating enough that I knew you'd want to know about it," Torr murmured.

"Of course," Ward replied, shrugging.

"Ward," Abby put in, "I still think we can avoid having to tell Cynthia. Torr believes we ought to pull the blackmailer's teeth by removing the threat, but I'm sure if we just put our minds to it the three of us can deal with this. As soon as we know the extortionist's demands, we'll have a better idea of who and what we're up against. Cynthia doesn't ever have to know about this."

"I think," Torr stated deliberately, "that it would be best if Cynthia knew everything. It's the only way to free Abby completely."

"No!" Abby snapped her head around, glaring at him. "I agreed to talk to Ward but that's as far as it goes. I don't want Cynthia in on this."

"You will do as I think best in this situation, Abby," Torr said quietly, every word utterly calm and utterly certain. "I've had a lot more experience with the criminal mind than you have. Remember that corporate mentality we discussed?"

"You're not going to make this decision for me, Torr Latimer!" she hissed.

"Actually," Ward interjected coolly before Torr could respond, "it's my decision to make and I've already made it. I made it the day I returned from that stupid weekend. I told Cynthia everything that afternoon."

9

ABBY PALED. Eyes riveted to Ward's face, she sat frozen for a moment. "You did what?" she finally got out weakly.

"I explained everything to her," Ward said evenly. "Told her what a fool I'd been and how I'd tried to involve you in my foolishness. If you want the truth, I think she already knew it all, anyway."

"You're joking! But . . . but she's been as close to me as ever! She never gave any indication that she knew you and I . . . that we . . ."

"We never did anything, did we, Abby? That's the part you're supposed to remember. What's more, you never would have had an affair with me. Perhaps subconsciously I realized that all along. In a way you were 'safe' for me. I'm not proud of what happened, but it wasn't the end of the world as far as Cynthia was concerned. She forgave me completely."

"Your wife sounds like a very generous woman," Torr observed.

"My wife is an incredible person and she loves me." Ward spoke simply. "What's more, I love her. I always have and I always will. I went a little crazy there for a while. It won't ever happen again."

Abby absorbed the implications of his statement. In the midst of the turmoil she was experiencing the only thing that stood out clearly was a sudden, heartfelt desire to have Torr Latimer declare such words of love. Forever words.

"Well," said Torr smoothly, "that does unmuddy the waters a little."

"What do you suggest now?" Ward seemed quite willing to accept the other man as an equal. It spoke volumes for the respect he must have felt. That surprised Abby at first. And then she realized that her cousin's husband was anything but a stupid man. He would know his match when he saw him.

"I think we'll just wait for the payoff demand. Then we'll take it to the police together with our suspicions," Torr said flatly.

"There's another possibility," Ward mused.

"A private investigator?" Torr nodded thoughtfully. Abby was beginning to feel very much left out of the conversation.

"Why do we want a private investigator?" she asked.

"He might have more luck finding out who's behind the blackmail attempt," Torr explained politely.

"Just who is it you suspect?" Ward demanded.

"Oh, Torr has some ridiculous notion that Flynn Randolph might be behind all this," Abby said dismissively. "He fits the 'profile.'"

"What profile?" Ward pressed.

"One Torr has been compiling from what little we know."

"Randolph is only one of several possibilities," Torr interrupted calmly. "I rather like the idea of an investigator at this point. Know a good agency?"

"One of the best. I'm using them on something else at the moment. I'll give them a call this afternoon."

Abby looked from one to the other and decided that whatever happened next was out of her hands. Men. They thought they could run the world. "Ward, what was it that you wanted to see me about this past week?"

Ward pulled himself back from the conversation he had begun with Torr, glancing at her quickly. "Business, as I said. Someone's buying up shares of our stock. Since you hold the largest single block outside of Cynthia's portion, I wanted to get to you and warn you that you will probably be approached with an offer."

Abby was startled. "But, Ward, you know I'd never sell. And certainly not without discussing the matter with you and Cynthia. Besides, the shares aren't worth much."

Ward ran a hand through his brown hair and smiled grimly. "The offers have been surprisingly lucrative. Aunt May and Uncle Harold sold theirs last week without bothering to consult me. Said they had no idea I might be upset."

"But this has always been a family company."

"Well, it's not going to be in a couple of months. I'm taking the firm public, Abby."

"You're going to sell the stock on the open market? Why?"

It was Torr who answered. "Quickest way for a small firm to acquire a lot of capital. Issue stock and sell it on the open market. Instant cash, providing there are some willing buyers."

"There will be plenty of those when we unveil our latest bit of technology," Ward said.

"So someone's trying to get in on the ground floor by buying up what's now in family hands, right?" Torr smiled fleetingly, the expression rather predatory.

"He could acquire enough to give him a tremendous amount of control. He will also become very rich overnight when the stock goes public."

"Who is it?" Abby interposed quickly.

"I don't know yet. The offers have come through an intermediary. A third party who claims he's representing an interested businessman. Finding out who that 'interested businessman' is is the task I have the investigative agency on at the moment."

"Hell." Torr's comment was succinct and not unsympathetic.

"Isn't it, though," Ward agreed gruffly. "I feel better now that I've finally caught up with Abby and had a chance to warn her."

"Are a lot of the other relatives selling?" Abby demanded, infuriated at the notion.

"Unfortunately I haven't been able to convince all of Cynthia's relatives that if they want to sell, they should at least wait until we go public. They'll get a lot more for the stock then. But they're so accustomed to the idea of the company bordering on the edge of bankruptcy that they're welcoming offers. I guess they don't believe I'll pull the firm out of the red."

"Well, you won't lose my stock!" Abby declared forcefully.

"Thanks." Ward grinned. "I needed to hear that. I wasn't sure just how much faith you had in me these days. Especially after what happened two months ago."

Abby leaned forward impulsively, putting out her hand to cover Ward's fingers. "Ward, I've never doubted your ability to handle the firm. What's more, I've always had a lot of faith in you as a man. You've made Cynthia very happy."

Abruptly Torr got to his feet. He closed his large hand around Abby's wrist and pointedly removed her comforting fingers from Ward's. "I think that's about enough family sympathy and support," he remarked. "It's all very touching, naturally, but for my peace of mind, I'd like to limit just how touching. Come on, Abby, you and I are going to get a cup of coffee while Ward calls that investigation agency." He glanced at a wryly amused Ward. "See if they can get someone over here reasonably soon. I'd like to get back to Portland in the morning."

Ward nodded. "I'll get on it now. And, Abby?"

"Yes, Ward?" Abby was already half out of the office because of Torr's firm grip on her wrist.

"I'm sorry. For everything."

"So am I, Ward." She got no further. Torr was in the act of closing the office door behind them before she could finish the sentence.

In silence he guided her through the outer office, nodding politely if distantly at the middle-aged secretary who smiled back in mild puzzlement. Then Abby found herself in a crowded elevator descending to the lobby. It wasn't until she was seated across from Torr in the glassed-in sidewalk café on the ground floor of the building that Abby finally got a chance to free her wrist. She favored Torr with a scathing glance of pure annoyance.

"You didn't have to manhandle me like that! You know perfectly well by now that there was never anything between Ward and myself and there never will be. I was merely being sympathetic. He's under a lot of pressure."

"Comforting a man when he's in that state can lead to all sorts of problems. I'd have thought you'd have learned that by now. It was how you got into trouble last time with Ward, remember?" Torr eyed her sardonically, stirring his coffee with an absent gesture.

Abby blinked in sudden wariness. "But nothing happened. You know that."

"But you were willing to submit to blackmail to keep your cousin Cynthia from finding out that nothing happened, weren't you?"

"Torr! Are you saying you don't believe me?" she whispered tightly.

"No. I believe you." His face softened appreciably as he saw the stricken look in her blue eyes. "But that doesn't mean I'm going to let you run around comforting every male in the vicinity who happens to be under a lot of stress. If you want to comfort someone, comfort me. I trust you, honey, but I'm not about to let your impulsiveness lead you into any more untenable situations. Clear?"

"You've gotten awfully bossy lately, Torr." Abby's eyes narrowed. "On second thought, I guess you were all along. Wonder why I didn't notice it right off?"

Torr said nothing, merely smiled gently and plucked the daisy from the small glass bud vase in the center of the table. He extended his palm toward her, the daisy lying across it. His amber eyes gleamed with silent urging.

Abby eyed the daisy and then looked up at the man offering it. There was no doubt that he was reminding her of the night she had taken the yellow rose from his hand and found herself in bed with him. A shiver of love and sensual anticipation gripped her as the memories flooded into her head.

"Do you think," she began in a tight whisper, "that flowers will get you anything you want?"

"I only want you."

Abby bit her lip and then made a quick grab for the daisy. Snatching it up, she carried it down under the table, cradling it in her lap. She refused to meet his eyes for some time after that, fully aware that she would find nothing but masculine satisfaction reflected in the golden pools. She could do without that for a while, she thought with a small smile.

THE INTERVIEW with the investigator sent over by the agency was not at all what Abby had anticipated. She'd read enough detective fiction to know what private eyes ought to look like and this one didn't fit the mold at all. He was dressed like an executive, spoke in a well-educated manner, and took notes with a tape recorder. The recorder made Abby uneasy, but the man's careful questioning eventually drew out everything she knew or guessed. While her own answers were somewhat hesitant, Torr and Ward spoke as easily as if they had prepared written reports. Executives, she thought grimly, right down to their toenails. They were succinct, crisp, organized and didn't seem fazed by some of the more embarrassing aspects of the situation.

"Not what you expected, Abby?" Torr asked with lazy amusement after the investigator had departed.

"Obviously the man has not read Raymond Chandler," she sniffed.

"Or maybe he has and decided to upgrade the image," Ward suggested. "Whatever the reason for the style, the agency's good."

"You said earlier you have them looking into the stock purchases?" Torr asked curiously.

"Ummm. I want to know who's out there buying up the family stock, and what's more, I want to know how he knew it was suddenly becoming available."

"He must have someone inside," Torr observed thoughtfully.

"I'm afraid so."

"A spy? In the company?" Abby asked, horrified.

"Just someone who's trying to make a few bucks on the side peddling company information," Ward replied, shrugging. "Happens a lot these days."

"That's disgusting. Thank heavens I don't have to deal with that sort of thing in my vitamin business."

"There are advantages to being self-employed." Torr chuckled. "I know how you feel."

"You two seem to have a few things in common," Ward said, grinning.

"More than you will ever know," Torr said.

"So how is business, Abby?" Ward turned to her, leaning back in his chair.

"Judging by the amount of pills she takes every day, business has got to be booming." Torr stepped in to answer for her.

"Go ahead and laugh," Abby challenged. "I haven't had a cold in almost a year."

Ward looked at Torr. "Better prepare yourself for a lifetime of good health."

Abby flushed at the use of the word "lifetime." She and Torr had made no lasting commitments of any kind, but she hardly wanted to explain that to Ward. Torr took the comment easily enough, however, smiling as he glanced at Abby.

"The woman's worth a few pills," he said blandly.

"Gee, thanks." Abby rose from her chair disdainfully. "If the two of you are through playing detective, I think I'd like to do some shopping."

"I'll call Cynthia and warn her you'll be coming over for dinner," Ward said, reaching for the phone.

"No!" Hastily Abby turned back, an anxious expression on her face. "No, Ward, I'd rather not. I mean, not this trip. Perhaps another time. I don't want to have to explain. I mean, it would just be too awkward and she's got her hands full with the baby and all—"

"Abby," Torr interrupted calmly, catching her restlessly waving wrist, "calm down. Ward says she knows everything, remember?"

"But I didn't know she knew everything," Abby wailed beseechingly.

"Cynthia and you are like sisters. If she was going to have any lasting problems about that idiotic incident, you'd know it by now," Ward pointed out coolly, dialing his home number.

He was right, Abby realized gloomily. But how could she explain that she was going to feel strange sitting down to dinner with Cynthia, knowing that her cousin knew all about that embarrassing weekend? She thought back to all the phone calls she'd had with Cynthia since the baby's birth, remembered going to see her in the hospital. Cynthia had known everything then and yet her affection for Abby had undergone no change.

"Abby, will you stop feeling guilty?" Torr growled gently. "You did nothing wrong. Cynthia is aware of that." He got up and nodded at Ward. "We'll see you for dinner. Seven o'clock?"

"Fine. Laura will be in bed by then."

Torr escorted Abby out of the office before she could think of any further arguments. Actually, she acknowledged wryly, both men were right. There was no reason at all why she shouldn't be looking forward to having dinner with Cynthia and Ward. She'd enjoyed dinner with both of them often enough in the past. So why was she feeling so uncertain and upset about it?

"Are you really that nervous about facing your cousin?" Torr led her to the elevator and down to the parking garage.

"I can't explain it," Abby sighed as she let him stuff her gently into the BMW.

"Can't you?" he asked as he started the car and headed for the exit.

"Will you stop being so cryptic?" she flared, thoroughly annoyed. "What's that supposed to mean? I should think my reasons for being anxious about seeing Cynthia are obvious!"

"You just said you couldn't explain them. How can they be obvious?" Torr paused to pay the parking lot attendant and then pulled out into the stream of traffic.

"You're deliberately trying to bait me," she accused frostily.

Torr shook his head once. "No, I'm only trying to find out something."

"Then ask. Don't use devious tactics."

"Okay, I'll ask. Are you nervous about meeting Cynthia again because mentally and emotionally you're putting yourself in her place? Are you imagining what it would be like if you were Cynthia and were fixing dinner for the woman your husband tried to take to bed a couple of months ago?"

Abby drew in her breath, glaring out the window at the shops and buildings along Fourth Avenue. "Your logic is appalling."

"But is it accurate?"

"Why do you want to know?"

"Maybe I'd like to know if the reason you find yourself empathizing with Cynthia is because you've gotten to the point where you might be capable of a little jealousy."

"About who?" she demanded.

"Me?" he suggested hopefully.

She turned to stare at his unreadable profile. Quite suddenly something clicked into place, sliding home in her subconscious like a knife into a sheath. "There would be no need, would there?" she whispered.

"No need?"

"I mean, I might or might not feel jealousy, but there would be no need. Not with you. Not if you had made a commitment."

He shrugged. "Maybe that's how Cynthia feels about Tyson now."

"But in her case there was a . . . a problem."

"Maybe they used the problem to resolve some things. Important things."

"Perhaps." Abby began to relax a bit at the thought. "Ward certainly seemed committed this afternoon."

"I don't know why you doubt your cousin's trust. You've certainly shown a lot more trust in me than most women would have under the circumstances."

Abby considered that. "And you've done the same with me."

"We'll have to pursue this interesting discussion to its logical conclusion very soon," Torr remarked as he pulled the BMW into the drive of one of the big downtown hotels.

"Why are we stopping here?" Abby glanced around, suddenly aware of their destination.

"Because, while I'm more than willing to meet members of your family, I'm going to want you to myself later." Torr parked the car and opened the door. "I'm going to check in. Be back in a moment."

Abby chewed her lip thoughtfully, watching as Torr disappeared behind the opulent glass doors of the hotel lobby. There was nothing in particular to be said. Later she was going to want him to herself, too.

She might as well face the fact that she had embarked on an affair. An affair with the man she loved. The only question remaining was how did Torr feel about her. Protective? Certainly. Attracted? Definitely. Committed? Possibly. In love?

There was no answer for that one, she realized. She wouldn't know until he said it or until he came close to saying it by asking her to marry him. Torr Latimer had been very badly burned once by marriage. He wasn't likely to risk it so soon again. What in the world was she doing considering marriage to this man? A man she had met only a couple of weeks before. A man who was demonstrating few if any of the characteristics she had once told herself she wanted in a man. Oh, he had started out all right, she thought wryly. Restrained, amenable, polite. But he had certainly shown his true colors this week and they included a tendency to dominate and overwhelm when the occasion arose.

He also had this thing about flowers.

It was the thing about flowers that Cynthia remembered. She opened the door of her Mercer Island home to them and stared straight up at Torr, blue eyes alive with fascination.

"This is the one you met in the class of Japanese flower arrangement?" she demanded of Abby.

"Yes," said Abby with a smile.

"You were right. He is a viable candidate."

Abby went red in a way she hadn't done since childhood. "Cynthia!"

Torr's arm draped heavily around her shoulders as he flashed an exceedingly wicked, rather satisfied grin. "I'm flattered. I had no idea I ranked so high in your estimation. What, precisely, am I a candidate for?"

"Never mind," Abby muttered as she stepped into the spacious hallway and allowed Cynthia to close the door.

"I've been trying to get Abby interested in someone for almost two years," Cynthia said. "Seriously interested. It's been a hopeless task. I had this wonderful vice president in mind. He works for Ward. But I can see now that it won't be necessary to introduce him to Abby."

"Not necessary at all," Torr agreed with a thread of steel in his voice. His grip tightened visibly, although his smile remained bland.

"Dear me, the possessive type." Cynthia chuckled as she led the way into the step-down living room where Ward was fixing drinks at the bar. "I didn't think Abby went for that type. Not since she had a rather nasty experience with someone a couple of years back."

"I'm afraid I haven't given Abby much choice in the matter," Torr confided.

"Can I see Laura?" Abby put in aggressively in a desperate bid to change the topic of conversation.

"This way," Cynthia told her, laughing and leaving Ward and Torr to greet each other.

Abby followed her cousin's blond artfully tousled head as she led the way to the white-and-yellow nursery. Cynthia had already regained much of her formerly excellent figure and there was a healthy glow about her that had been missing during much of her pregnancy. And the affection in her eyes when she smiled at Abby contained all of the familiar sisterly trust and love.

In silence they bent over the tiny shape in the crib. Baby Laura was sleeping peacefully, her little fingers curled beside her cheek. For a long moment Abby simply stared down at the infant, a little in awe of the small life form. There was a strange peace in the shadowy nursery that seemed to sink into Abby. When she glanced up at Cynthia she saw it mirrored in her cousin's smiling eyes. All of a sudden Abby was certain everything was all right between herself and Cynthia.

She was certain of something else, too. Torr had been right this afternoon in the car. She had begun putting herself emotionally in Cynthia's place. For the first time in her life she had known the potential for a woman's jealousy, and the man at its core was Torr Latimer.

Abby didn't kid herself. She knew that what she felt toward Torr was a form of raw possessiveness. She also knew it was illogical. She had no real right to feel that way and if she ever did obtain a genuine commitment from Torr, she would never have to worry about being given a cause for jealousy. The man could be trusted to the ends of the earth. Abby knew that with an instinct that defied description.

But that didn't negate the possessiveness she experienced around Torr. She understood now what the real thing meant. It was not the sick, mindless jealousy she had witnessed in Flynn Randolph. Instead it was a manageable, controlled emotion that was part of her love for Torr. It was all wrapped up with a woman's pride and passion. Perhaps it was the same for a man. A matter of pride and passion and love. Not at all the sick emotion of a Flynn Randolph.

"You look as if you've just had a revelation or two," Cynthia whispered with a smile as they stepped back out into the gray-carpeted hall and headed toward the living room.

"Revelations are notoriously difficult to explain," Abby murmured in response. "But I've had more than one while hanging around Torr Latimer."

"You're in love, aren't you?" Cynthia said with quiet knowledge.

"Does it show?"

"Very plainly to someone who knows you as well as I do. Have you told Torr?"

Abby shook her head. "I think he knows, though." She remembered the previous evening when he had told her he thought she could be controlled through love. He had meant that her love for him made her controllable.

"Take my advice, Abby. Don't ever depend on a man knowing of your love for him. You've got to tell him. They're a little dense in some ways."

"Men?"

"Charming creatures but not always at their brightest in the bedroom."

Abby stared at her cousin and then burst out laughing. After a moment Cynthia joined her, and the last of Abby's reserve vanished forever.

MUCH LATER that night Torr held Abby while she shimmered like hot gold in his arms. His raging desire fed on the response he had drawn from her, just as it always did, and even as she cried out his name in the breathless manner he craved, he was following her over the edge of passion and down into the depths of reality.

The pale lights of the city outside the hotel-room window cast magical shadows on the wide, rumpled bed and on the naked body of the woman he held. Her eyes remained closed for a long moment while she recovered her graceful strength and Torr gazed down into her face with a sense of wonder. He had been right when he had speculated that she would be like one of her own floral arrangements in bed. Wild, feminine chaos and excitement. Undisciplined and challenging at the beginning, warm and inviting at the end.

"What are you thinking?" Abby murmured from the curve of his arm.

"That I don't seem to get tired of rearranging you."

"You still think of me as a bunch of flowers?" She giggled, stretching sensuously beside him. Her left breast moved against his bare chest and Torr couldn't resist reaching out to stroke the pink tip.

"A bunch of flowers just waiting for the touch of a master floral designer," he teased, bending over to put his lips to her throat.

"You do seem to be getting awfully skilled at it," she sighed, arching her neck for him. Her honey hair fanned out in abandon on the pillow.

"It's becoming a habit," Torr admitted, finding all the warm, vulnerable places on her throat. The scent of her body in the aftermath of lovemaking was enough to arouse him all over again. "And I think we should discuss the matter."

"The habit?"

"Ummm. Abby, when we go back to Portland, we're not going back to the slow cautious relationship we had there."

He felt her tense at the determination in his voice but he refused to back off. Some things had to be made clear now, tonight.

"What are you suggesting, Torr?"

He shut his eyes, aware of the delicious feel of her fingers in his hair. It was now or never. He'd put it off this long but he couldn't put it off any longer. "I want you to come and live with me, Abby."

As if she had been waiting for another answer, he felt her body stiffen and then go very still beneath him.

"I'll . . . I'll think about it, Torr."

His fingers tightened on her shoulders as he lifted his head to stare down into her face. "There's nothing to think about," he said, incensed at her hesitancy even though he had half expected it. "You're moving in with me and that's all there is to it."

She stirred beneath him. "This isn't something you can achieve by sheer force of will. I told you I'll think about it."

"It's not as if I'm asking you to marry me," he rasped.

"No, it's not as if you're asking me to marry you."

Torr stared down at her. If his very soul had depended on it, he could not have read her expression in that moment. "When we get back to Portland, I'll be staying with you in any case," he tried to point out logically. "I'll be living with you until this blackmail mess is cleared up."

"Will you?"

"Yes! Abby, we've been living together for the past week, anyway. Why the hell are you acting like this tonight? You want me. I know you want me."

"Yes," she breathed huskily, her nails sliding persuasively around his shoulders. "I want you." She pulled his dark head down to hers, opening her mouth for him in a way that forced him to respond. She was like a handful of flowers. A whole bunch of them. Lush roses, pert daisies, exotic orchids. Torr couldn't resist losing himself in the scent and feel of the petals that beckoned.

Tomorrow, he promised himself as he drank honey from her mouth and ran his hand down her body to find the honey between her thighs. Tomorrow he would make it clear that she had no choice. She was going to come and live with him.

Long after Torr was sprawled in sleep beside her, Abby lay awake staring out the window at the gleaming night. Why had she thought that he would propose marriage? Hadn't she told herself only recently that Torr had been badly burned in marriage and would not jump into another one?

Why did she want marriage from him in the first place, she wondered. Because it was a sign of commitment, she realized. A sign that he not only trusted her, but that he loved her.

What on earth had she expected after only a week or so of really being together? What a fool she had been. Of course the man needed time. So did she, if she was realistic about it. Both of them were just starting out on the long road of a serious relationship. Marriage was a hasty move at this point. Torr's suggestion was much more sensible.

He had taken her by surprise tonight. That was the whole problem. She had just returned from an evening in which she'd been pleasantly surrounded by domestic harmony. Babies and a home and a commitment between two people had all combined to leave her feeling a lack in her own life.

She had known with sure instinct that Torr Latimer could fill that lack and that he was the only man who could. With him she yearned for a home and a commitment and a future. When he had spoken of living together she had been willing him to speak of something more definite. Talk about learning the meaning of possessiveness! She wanted some sign that he was falling in love with her, that he cared for her as much as she cared for him. That he needed her as much as she needed him.

He's turned my whole life upside down, she thought. A few days before she wouldn't have even wanted to discuss marriage with any man. Ruefully, Abby smiled in the darkness.

The thing to remember, she told herself, was that by demanding that she live with him, Torr Latimer was making a commitment. He wouldn't have suggested anything so binding as that kind of agreement unless he was willing to live up to his side of it. His marriage had been a disaster and it stood to reason that he would be far more cautious the second time around.

Why was she hesitating? Afraid of giving up her personal freedom for an indefinite commitment? What a fool she was. She loved this man. No risk was too great. Given time he could fall in love with her. Really in love.

Abby turned on her side and reached out to shake Torr awake. Her nails bit gently into his shoulder and she heard him mumble a sleepy protest.

"What the . . . ?" He shifted slowly onto his back, gazing at her with lazy, half-closed eyes. "What's the matter, flower? Do you want to be arranged again?" His voice was thick with affection and sleep.

"I woke you up to tell you that I've decided to live with you when we get back to Portland," she murmured, trying to search his face in the shadows.

There was silence from him but it was a watchful silence. He was suddenly very awake behind those hooded eyes, Abby realized. And even though he made no move, she knew his body was coming alert.

She never did get a verbal response. The next thing Abby knew she was lying flat on her back, crushed into the bedding by a familiar beloved weight. Torr's body covered her with passionate aggression and she gave herself up to the enthralling depths of his desire.

10

TO ABBY'S SURPRISE and wry amusement, Torr was extremely agreeable the next day. He agreed to begin their new living arrangements in her apartment when she explained that she ran her business from there and it would take time to move it. He agreed to take her to lunch on the wharf before they left Seattle and he agreed to let her drive the BMW part of the way back to Portland.

"Why?" was all he asked when she made the last request.

"Because I've never driven a foreign car."

"Oh." But he was extremely gallant about the matter, nevertheless. She knew he didn't entirely relax, however, until they were out of the city traffic, heading south on Interstate 5.

"What's so amusing?" he inquired several miles down the road.

"I was thinking how amenable you've been today."

He flicked her an assessing glance. "Satisfied males tend to be amenable."

"Really? Are you satisfied?"

"Almost."

"Ah, you mean you won't be entirely satisfied until I'm living in your house, right?" she ventured curiously.

He shrugged. "Where we live isn't all that important. Spending a couple of weeks in your apartment while you work on transferring your business arrangements to my house isn't a problem. I like your apartment."

"Do you? Why?"

"Because it has you written all over it, I imagine."

"I know," she said, sighing, "undisciplined, impulsive, haphazard . . ."

"And soft and warm and interesting," he finished firmly. "Look, I know this is going to seem rather staid and conventional of me, but I feel I should take this opportunity to remind you that there is a speed limit in this state."

"Oh, yes?"

"You're exceeding it," he pointed out very politely.

"A little too much excitement for you?"

"I'm afraid so," he murmured blandly. "Pull over. I'll drive."

"So much for your amenability," she groaned.

THEY ARRIVED IN Portland in the late afternoon. The bridges into the heart of the city were jammed with rush-hour traffic and instead of fighting it, Torr pulled into the parking lot of a florist and disappeared inside. Abby watched him go, smiling to herself. What kind of flowers would Torr select this time?

When he returned he carried a small bunch sheathed in plastic and a low jade-green bowl. "Knowing your taste in flower arrangements, I doubt if you have anything really appropriate to arrange these in so I bought a bowl and a frog, too."

They stopped at another point and bought groceries. It was beginning to feel very settled and comfortable, this business of shopping with Torr, Abby decided as she selected mushrooms and pea pods. Almost a married feeling.

But not quite. She realized she was getting possessive. She wanted it all.

By the time they had stored the groceries in the back of the BMW, the traffic had cleared and they made their way downtown to Abby's apartment building.

"I don't know how you do it," she marveled as Torr found his usual parking spot on the street in front. "The odds against finding a place right here must be a million to one."

"I guess I just live right."

They carried the suitcases and the groceries and the flowers to the elevator and then down the hall to Abby's door. As soon as she rounded the corner, Abby saw the sheaf of delivery notices hanging on the doorknob.

"Oh, dear, I hope the vitamins all got delivered okay," she said worriedly, fishing out her key. They were stacked just inside the door, several green-and-gold boxes filled with bottles of tablets. There was also a variety of notes from the saleswoman she had left in charge, explaining what she had taken to fill the orders of the rest of the sales force.

"Do these boxes arrive all the time? Day in and day out?" Torr asked curiously.

"I'm afraid so. I need constant shipments to keep up with the demand."

"I should think there would be a more efficient way of handling the deliveries," he pointed out, frowning.

"What could be more efficient than having them delivered to my door?" she demanded in astonishment.

"At least at my place I have a spare room to stack the boxes in," Torr said, shoving a carton aside with his foot as he made his way into the kitchen.

"I should never have been gone so long," Abby said apprehensively, scanning the notes that were stacked on the nearest box. "Looks like there've been a few problems."

"You had problems of your own," Torr reminded her grimly as he unpacked groceries. "And they're not over yet."

She looked up sharply from the note she was reading. "But that private investigator will clear it up, won't he?"

"I think so," Torr said reassuringly. "The blackmailer may back off of his own accord if he realizes we've neutralized his threat."

"I still want to know who it is and why he's doing it. I just can't believe it could be Flynn. It doesn't make any sense." Abby shook her head as she started toward the bedroom to change her clothes.

Torr didn't answer her and she knew he had his own theories on the subject. Instinctively she felt that those theories were inspired by his dislike of the way Randolph had treated her. Torr's reaction was protective and very male but not necessarily logical. As Abby pulled off the cream knit sheath she had worn home from Seattle and selected a pair of jeans and a jewel-plaid shirt, she could hear water running in the kitchen. She wondered if Torr was starting dinner. He had said something earlier about running up to his house and getting some fresh clothes. Abby slipped into a pair of sandals and padded curiously back out to the kitchen.

Torr was industriously at work arranging the flowers he had bought in the jade-green bowl. He didn't glance up as Abby came to a halt in the doorway, and she smiled wistfully at his intentness. Watching him reminded her of the first time she had seen him in class.

"Couldn't wait to start arranging, hmmm?" she teased.

"I didn't want the flowers to dry out while I drive over to my place. Also," he added gently, "I didn't want you getting your hands on them first."

"No faith!"

"Oh, I have faith that you'd create an arrangement, but it wouldn't be quite the right one for this bowl. The flowers would wind up going every which way and you wouldn't have enough to work with anyhow, would you? You were always running short in class. Besides, this is supposed to be a gift to you from me."

"You know what I think? I think you wanted to create a nice severe sort of arrangement in an attempt to counter the chaos of this apartment." She glanced around at all the vitamin boxes and groaned. "I'll try and get some of those packages off the floor and into a closet while you're gone."

He frowned. "I was going to take you with me while I picked up my things." Very carefully he adjusted a stately yellow gladiolus so that it perfectly balanced the low orchid.

"I'd rather stay here and get dinner going and arrange these vitamin boxes. Don't worry, I won't mess up your flower arrangement."

"Well, I suppose it will be all right. I'll only be gone for an hour or so." He smiled wryly. "I'm getting used to not letting you out of my sight."

"If you're worried about the blackmailer, it's safe to say that the one thing he hasn't done is show himself in person," Abby pointed out logically. "He's not likely to start now."

"No." Torr arranged another little orchid with meticulous care. Then he selected a tall green leaf and arranged it as a backdrop for the gladiolus and the orchids. In all he used only three flowers and a leaf. Apparently satisfied, he stepped back to survey the creation.

"You've still got some flowers left over," Abby frowned.

"The trick is knowing where to stop."

"But what about over there on the right? You could stuff in a couple more glads and maybe a little daisy or something. It looks a little bare."

"It looks serene," Torr declared. "Mrs. Yamamoto would approve, I think."

Abby narrowed her eyes speculatively. "I still think a little more yellow in that corner would be nice."

"And then you'd want to add a little more gold over there and another leaf or two or three. Here. You can play with the rest of these leftover flowers while I'm gone."

"Okay." She accepted them eagerly.

"But not in my bowl," he added severely. "Find your own."

"I think I could really beef up the arrangement you've started," she argued. "All it needs is a few final touches—"

Torr silenced her with his fingertips across her mouth. Then he bent down and dropped a kiss on the top of her head. "Abby, honey, there are only two things I require of you during the next hour. One, you will not open the door to anyone, and two, you will keep your hands off my flower arrangement. Understood?"

"You never let me have any fun," she replied. But he didn't look nearly so grim these days, Abby thought contentedly as he picked up his jacket and headed for the door. In fact, with a little imagination, she could say he almost looked like a man in love. Or falling in love. Maybe very close to falling in love. What did a man look like when he was in love? The door closed behind him.

Abby stood staring thoughtfully for a long moment and then she became aware of the flowers in her hands. Automatically she glanced over at the jade-green bowl with its stylized arrangement. Dutifully she reminded herself not to get any ideas and decided to put temptation out of the way. She carried the bowl into the living room and set it down on the smoked-glass coffee table. It really was an elegant arrangement, she decided. Elegant and strong.

Of course, a bit more yellow and gold on the right side wouldn't be amiss, Abby told herself. Ah, well, no sense starting off her new domestic life on the wrong foot. Virtuously she carried her flowers into the kitchen and stuck them at satisfyingly wild angles into a glass vase. Then she set about restacking and arranging vitamin boxes.

It was while she was shifting a carton of vitamin C tablets that she realized she had been recently forgetting to take her daily supplements. The thought made her smile. Something about Torr Latimer lent strength and vitality enough to her life. She didn't seem to need so many vitamins with him around.

She was trying to stack three boxes of multiple vitamins on top of a high mound of mineral supplements when the doorbell chimed. The boxes cascaded to the floor and she kicked at them disgustedly as she went to answer the door.

"Who is it?" Abby wiped her perspiring forehead on her sleeve.

"Consolidated Delivery Service," came back the laconic answer.

"Oh, lord! More boxes. Just what I need." Dismayed, Abby stalked across the room and yanked open the door.

"You guys are certainly working late this evening. Couldn't you have saved this delivery for tomorrow? I don't even have enough room to store—Oh, my God."

The last three words came out very slowly and evenly as she finally realized who was standing outside her door.

"Hello, Abby. It's been a long time."

Flynn Randolph was inside the apartment before she could even think of trying to get the door shut. He wrenched her hand off the knob with a touch of the violence she remembered so well, and then he smiled. It was the kind of smile she had once thought handsomely sardonic and had eventually realized hid a menace that was not governed by logic or self-control.

"Don't scream, darling. My temper is a little short at the moment. You remember my temper? You used to complain about it a great deal there toward the end." His fingers slid around her throat and he pressed just enough to remind her of their last encounter. The one in which he'd lost his control completely and struck her.

"What are you doing here, Flynn?" With an effort of will Abby kept her voice calm as she moved out of his grip and stepped back. Staying calm was the only way she knew to handle him.

"I thought it was time you and I renewed old acquaintances, sweet whore. Come on, Abby. You were never dumb. You know why I'm here."

"You're the one who's been sending the pictures, aren't you?" She tried to speak easily, as if they were involved in only a casual conversation.

"Of course." He smiled and there was an unnatural excitement in his dark eyes. "You thought you could hide out with your latest lover, didn't you? But he's gone now. I watched him leave. He brought you back home and dumped you, didn't he? Knowing what you are must have made him sick. You're lucky he didn't do to you what he did to his wife. I remembered that story. I remembered it very well when I found out who had taken you away to the Columbia River gorge. A little research in the public library turned up the clippings. Bet that put a scare into you, didn't it? Finding out you'd sought refuge with a murderer?"

"He's not a murderer and he'll be back soon, Flynn."

"You're lying, bitch." The evil smile disintegrated. "He's dumped you. I've been watching your apartment for the past couple of days. I knew it was only a matter of time before he dropped you off. Where were you going to run next?"

Apparently Flynn did not know about the side trip to Seattle, Abby thought. He didn't realize that his extortion scheme might have been neutralized.

"Your threats aren't worth anything, Flynn. My cousin knows all about that weekend at the beach."

His smile returned. "Abby, Abby. Why are you lying like this? The last thing you would want is to have Cynthia find out what a slut you really are. We both know that. And that's why you and I are going to talk a little business tonight."

His fingers caressed the nape of her neck in a subtle threat as he guided her over toward the sofa and pushed her into a sitting position. He stood close, too close.

Abby didn't dare move for fear of provoking real violence. Perhaps if she just stayed very calm and kept him talking until Torr returned she could get through this unscathed. Flynn had been unpredictable toward the end of the period in which she had known him. She had no way of telling how much more violent or unpredictable he had become in the intervening two years.

She should never have opened the front door. Torr was not going to be pleased, Abby decided wryly.

"You haven't told me what you want, Flynn." With an outer coolness that amazed her, Abby sat primly on the edge of the sofa, looking up at him.

"Well, I sure don't want you, you little whore," he returned easily. "You really can't get enough, can you? You put on such an act with me, always saying you weren't ready for commitment, refusing to go to bed with me and all the while you were hopping into bed with anything in pants."

"That's not true, Flynn. You and I were never serious about each other."

"We were engaged!" he ground out.

"No, we were not engaged and you know it. You never had any claim on me, Flynn." Instantly Abby realized her mistake. He did not want to be contradicted. His dark eyes hardened dangerously and the face that had once seemed so good-looking became a mask of hate.

"You think I don't know what you were up to while we were engaged? You think I don't know about all the men you were seeing behind my back? You little bitch! Why don't you admit it?"

"What do you want from me, Flynn?" she repeated steadily.

He stared at her and then seemed to regain control of himself. Abby concealed a shiver. It had never been this precarious when she had known him. He seemed far more volatile now. Looking up at him, Abby could see that the potential for violence that she had begun to sense in him two years before, but had only witnessed once, was now flickering much closer to the surface. The man was very dangerous now.

"What kind of business?"

"Nothing too difficult for you to comprehend." He leaned over with unexpected swiftness, his fingers sliding back to her throat. Dark eyes burned with an unnatural brightness that was somehow more frightening than anything else about him. "I want the shares, Abby. The shares you own in your dear cousin's computer firm. You see, I have given this a lot of thought. I have hit upon the perfect revenge. You are going to make me a very rich man, whore."

"You're the one who's been trying to buy the family shares?" she got out in amazement. "But how did you know that the company's—" She broke off, not wanting to reveal more if he didn't already know it for himself.

"That Tyson's taking the company public? That he finally got it back on its feet and that when they do go public they will be announcing a major breakthrough in graphics programming? I know everything, Abby. Including how much control I'll have if I have your block of shares. You're going to sell them to me. For ten dollars," he concluded in satisfaction.

"How . . . how did you know all that?" Talking. She must keep him talking. Torr had said he'd be gone an hour and forty minutes had already passed.

"I've known where you were the past couple of years. Did you really think I'd let you get away with what you did to me two years ago? Oh, no. You had to be punished. I knew about your shares from the beginning, remember? You used to laugh at how worthless they were. You also told me that all the rest of the family had stock. But you didn't tell me how little each one held. I soon realized I was wasting my time approaching all the relatives individually. But I remembered that you held quite a chunk. Enough that, combined with whatever else I can pick up from all the sweet little aunts and uncles and nieces and nephews, will let me gain a seat on the board and a lot of control."

"And if I don't sell them to you for a nominal sum?" she prodded carefully.

"Why then I'll make sure that your sweet cousin Cynthia sees what a two-faced little bitch you are. I'll let her know how you seduced her husband. You saw those photos I took while you and he were rendezvousing at the coast last winter. How do you think she'll feel when she sees them? No." He shook his head with great certainty. "You'll never allow that to happen. You're too soft when it comes to Cynthia. Hard as nails when it comes to taking what you want from a man, but you're soft on your cousin. I know you, darling Abby. I know you very well."

Desperately she tried to get back to her earlier question. "All right, Flynn, I'll admit you know me well. But how did you find out about the firm's financial position? How did you know it was getting ready to go public?"

"I'm a businessman, remember?" he taunted. "I have a pipeline into your cousin's firm. I've had it for almost a year. I've been sitting back watching while Tyson pulled it out of the red. He's good, I'll agree to that. I have no objection to him staying on as president. But he's going to have to do things my way once I'm on the board. We're going to make a killing with that new graphics package. The stock's going to be worth a fortune on the open market. I'm going to be a very rich man when this is all over. You should have stuck with me, Abby. I could have made you the wife of a very rich man."

"You didn't love me, Flynn. You know that. You wanted to own me for some reason I could never quite fathom, but you didn't love me."

"Of course I didn't love you," he snarled. "How could any man love a tramp like you? But I wanted you," he went on seethingly. "You seduced me into wanting you. It was a deliberate game you played and then when you'd had your fill you walked off without a backward glance. Straight into the arms of a whole string of other men. But you're going to pay for your game. You're going to watch me sitting on Tyson's board, making decisions that affect your precious cousin and her husband and everyone else in the family. That's going to eat you up inside, isn't it? Knowing that you were the one who gave me control?"

"Flynn, believe me, I never tried to play games with you. You and I only dated for a few weeks. There never was any engagement and I never led you to believe I was falling in love with you."

"You lied to me! You deliberately toyed with me. But you're going to make up for it, Abby," he hissed. "You know how?"

"Flynn, stop it!"

"No, no, Abby, let me explain exactly how you're going to make up for being unfaithful. You're going to become my mistress."

She stared at him, dumbfounded. "Your mistress!"

"That's right," he nodded in satisfaction. "You're going to belong to me, body and soul. And you're going to be on your best behavior for as long as I want you because if you aren't, I'll use my seat on the board to ruin your precious cousin and everyone else in the family!"

Abby drew a shaky breath. "You need help, Flynn. Professional help. You're letting your bitterness toward me lead you into doing something terrible. You can't stoop to blackmail, for heaven's sake! Sooner or later you'll be—"

"Don't tell me what I can or can't do. I'm the one in charge now, Abby. I'm the one who gives the orders." He reached down swiftly and hauled her to her feet. She could feel his fingers bruising her arm through the plaid shirt, and in spite of her efforts to remain calm, Abby knew that fear was starting to take over in her body.

Panic welled up and it required a supreme effort of will to force it back under control.

"Flynn, please listen to me," she tried to say in a clear steady voice. "I'm not going to sell you the shares. Not for ten dollars or ten thousand dollars."

"Yes, you will." He shook her, eyes cold and not quite human. "You'll do anything to protect that cousin of yours."

"I might," Abby admitted truthfully, "but in this case it's not necessary. She knows all about that weekend on the coast. What's more she knows nothing happened between Ward and myself."

She'd made another mistake with that last sentence. A burning fury flared in Flynn Randolph's eyes and the hands on her arm dug deeper.

"You're lying!"

"No, it's true. She knows everything."

"If she does, then she knows you went to bed with her husband."

"I didn't."

"You little slut. I know all about it. I've been keeping an eye on you for the past six months. I know you met Tyson at the coast. I know you spent the night there with him. Don't try to tell me any different. I won't believe any more of your lies."

"You've been following me?" she gasped, horrified at the knowledge.

"Six months ago when I realized that Tyson's firm was probably going to make it and that there was a fortune to be had in the process, it occurred to me just how I could repay you for the way you treated me two years ago. Did you think I'd just forgive and forget the day you quit your job and disappeared? Did you?" He shook her, more viciously this time.

"You're a handsome, successful man, Flynn," Abby tried to point out reasonably. "You could probably have any woman you wanted—"

"Except you, right? Who the hell do you think you are to say I can't have you? I wanted you, Abby. Two years ago I'd have given you marriage. This time you'll come to me on my terms and you'll be sweet and obedient and you'll make every effort to keep me happy, won't you? Because if you don't I'll crucify your cousin and the family."

"You're irrational, Flynn."

"That's what they said to me at work," he startled her by admitting. "They said I was becoming irrational, that my decisions were arbitrary. But I'm going to show everyone. I'm going to have it all, a fortune and the woman who thought she was too good for me. In fact, little tease, I'm going to start claiming what's mine right now!"

"Flynn, no!"

He cut off her startled scream with the flat of his hand, slapping it savagely across her mouth as he pushed her onto the sofa. Abby panicked as she felt him tearing roughly at her clothing. The plaid shirt was ripped open with one violent movement, revealing her bra.

"I'll show you exactly what you are, whore!" He had gone over some inner edge. Abby could read it in his eyes. She was dealing with a man who was not only insane with fury, but probably insane, period.

Unable to shout or argue because of the sweating palm across her mouth, Abby struggled in fierce silence. She felt his hand on her body and her fear mingled with a rage unlike any she had ever known. She could not stand his touch and somewhere in the deepest recesses of her mind she realized suddenly why she had never been really tempted to drift into an affair with Flynn Randolph. She had known instinctively that he was wrong for her in every way. The surface charm that had once lured was now in tatters, and the irrational violent man underneath was all too evident.

The battle was vicious for all its silence. Abby could hear Flynn panting as he tried to anchor her to the sofa. His hot hand swept painfully over her breasts, trying to rip off the bra.

"Stop struggling, you little whore. This is what you live for. I'll give it to you better than you've ever had it. I'll make you beg for it. And when I've had enough of your begging, I'll take you until you cry out for mercy."

Abby shoved at him, raking her nails down his face and neck, trying to kick at him with her legs. He seemed oblivious to the pain she was inflicting, however, and she realized that she was not going to stand a chance of fighting him off. Wildly she struggled, managing to throw herself almost off the sofa.

She had lost all track of time now, had no idea when Torr might return. How long could she last? Flynn was so much stronger and his violence so irrational that she knew there was no hope of escaping.

Her hand flailed across the glass surface of the coffee table. Flynn's fingers were on the zipper of her jeans and she twisted with desperation. Once again her fingers scrabbled along the glass coffee table but this time they encountered an object. The jade-green bowl that contained Torr's elegant flower arrangement was where she had placed it earlier.

The bowl felt cool and hard beneath her touch, and all of a sudden Abby knew she held a weapon.

Abby could see the fire of the brilliant flowers out of the corner of her eye as she grasped the bowl and swung it in a short savage arc. How could there be such beauty in such savagery as she intended?

The bowl cracked against the side of Randolph's head with frightening force. Water and flowers cascaded over Flynn and Abby. The shock of the cold water made Abby catch her breath just as a hoarse primitive shout came from the doorway.

Abby barely had time to realize that it wasn't Flynn who had called out so violently before she found herself free of the oppressive weight of Flynn's collapsing body.

"Torr!"

He didn't even glance at her as he hauled the unconscious man off her and slung him down to the floor. Abby saw the way Torr's shoulders were bunched beneath the white fabric of the conservative shirt he wore. Feet apart, hands in knotted fists, he stood staring down at Flynn. Abby grabbed at her shirt, pulling it close around her and tried to catch her breath. Flowers lay strewn on the carpet and one of them lay crushed under Torr's heel.

"Oh, my God, Torr." She realized she was trembling, shaking as if she had a fever. "Oh, Torr."

He swung around then, apparently satisfied that the man on the floor wasn't going to move. Torr's amber eyes flared at her as savagely as had Flynn's. But although she was wary of this brand of savagery, Abby knew she didn't fear it in Torr. He was in control. There was a rational, if angry, intelligence governing his actions and she saw the difference between the two men as clearly as she could see the difference between night and day.

"How did he get in?" was all Torr asked, his voice tight and hard.

"I..." Abby licked her dry lips and tried again. "I thought he was the delivery man. I thought he was bringing another load of vitamins." Her voice sounded painfully weak, even to her own ears.

There was a deadly pause while Torr assimilated the vague excuse. "Are you all right?"

Startled not to be confronted with a severe lecture about having opened the door, Abby nodded mutely.

"Then call the police."

"Yes, Torr."

She was dialing the phone when Flynn groaned from his position on the floor and opened his eyes. Torr leaned over him.

"Move and I'll break your neck." The words were said with such dangerous calm that they penetrated even Flynn's dazed state. He looked up at Torr and then his furiously frustrated gaze sought out Abby.

"She should have been mine. I should have made her mine when I had the chance." Flynn groaned, his hand going to his bleeding scalp.

"He's not all there, Torr. He's sick." Abby spoke quietly as she waited for an answer on the other end of the line.

Torr glanced from the man at his feet to her anxious face. "I can see that. But sick or not, if he ever tries to go near you again, I'll kill him." He went down on his haunches beside the fallen man and stared into his stricken eyes. "Do you understand that, Randolph?"

"She's mine," Flynn hissed.

"No," Torr said evenly. "She belongs to me because she's given herself to me. Listen to me, Randolph, I will protect what is mine. If you ever go near her again, I'll kill you. Killing you would be easy for me. I've already killed in the past, remember?"

Flynn's eyes widened in comprehension. "Your wife. You killed your wife. I read about it in the newspaper. I remembered hearing about it at the time it happened. I never forgot that story. Never forgot it. Women can't be trusted." He sounded disoriented, his words vague and rambling as if he couldn't clear his thoughts. "A man can't trust them."

Torr reached down and put his fingers with awful care around Flynn's throat. "I trust Abby. I will trust her always. Nothing could destroy that trust. So if I find you near her again I will know that it wasn't because of anything Abby did. I will blame you entirely. Remember that, Randolph. I will blame you. And I will kill you."

Abby sat transfixed by the telephone, awed by the calm even violence in Torr's words. She felt the menace in him as if it were a tangible force, and it was becoming clear from the hypnotized expression in Flynn's eyes that he too felt the danger.

"You'll kill me," Flynn repeated dully.

"Yes."

He shook his head as if trying to clear away some of the pain and disorientation. "I won't come near her again. She's yours now."

"For the rest of her life," Torr said flatly.

"I won't hurt her. I won't go near her," Flynn promised as if he were a child. "Yours."

"Torr!"

Torr ignored Abby's husky interruption, focusing on Randolph as the man slipped into unconsciousness. Only when it was evident that Flynn was unable to hear him did he glance at Abby.

"Finish the call, Abby."

Obediently she did as she was told, her eyes never leaving Torr's grimly set face. When she finally set down the phone she was still struggling to find the right words. The flaring threat in his eyes was fading now and she took a deep breath.

"Why on earth did you enact that little scene with Flynn?" she whispered.

"A little basic psychology," Torr sighed, getting to his feet. "I want him afraid of me. Just in case the prison system in this country doesn't function properly. I want it impressed on his sick mind that coming near you means coming to his own death."

"More of your criminal psychology?" she demanded, watching as he bent down to pick up the flowers that had been scattered on the carpet. He handled each with a heart-stoppingly familiar care.

"I suppose so." He straightened, turning to face her with a bunch of flowers in his hand. "Abby?"

She saw the uncertainty in him and flew across the room and into his arms. "Of course I haven't changed my mind." Face buried against his shirt, she held him tightly around the waist. "I know perfectly well you didn't kill your wife."

"Abby, I could kill Randolph if I had to," Torr said carefully.

"I know."

"Does that frighten you?"

"No," she said simply. "You will do whatever is necessary in order to protect me."

"You sound as if you understand."

"I should." She lifted her face, her eyes glistening with tears of relief and love. "After all, I'd do whatever I had to do in order to protect you."

She felt him relax with a stifled groan as he tightened his arms around her. Any man was capable of violence under certain circumstances. So was any woman. Abby understood that now. But she would never fear Torr. The only kind of violence she would ever witness in him would be aimed at what threatened her. He would protect her but she would never be in real danger from him.

Perhaps she had subconsciously known that the first time she had seen him construct his serene, controlled masterpieces of floral design.

They held each other in gentle silence until the police arrived.

A LONG TIME LATER, after a talk with the police, a shower and a glass of wine, Abby sat in her bathrobe, her feet curled under her, regally prepared to listen to Torr's lecture. She could allow him to let off a little steam now that the disaster was all over. And she knew that as the situation had returned to normal so had Torr's temperament.

From across the room Torr watched her compose herself. One dark brow lifted quellingly. "I have a right to be a little upset, you know."

"Yes, Torr."

"I told you not to open that door to anyone, didn't I?"

"Yes, Torr."

"Are you going to sit there and say, 'yes, Torr' during this entire scene?"

"Yes, Torr."

"I ought to turn you over my knee," he groaned. There was a taut silence following that remark. "Aren't you going to say 'yes, Torr'?" he challenged silkily.

"I don't think so. Not to that particular remark."

"Abby, couldn't you follow one single little order?" he shot back roughly. "It was a simple enough set of instructions! But you couldn't do it, could you? Oh, no. You have to blithely throw open the door to the first guy who knocks. If you'd done as I told you, none of this would have happened."

"I realize that, Torr."

"Don't give me that meek little act," he rasped, beginning to pace up and down in front of her like an annoyed panther.

"Yes, Torr."

"This isn't a joke." He swung around, glowering at her.

"I know. I'm sorry. I don't know what to say. I just didn't think. He said he was the delivery service and I get so many deliveries I didn't stop to question it." Abby licked her lower lip and watched the man in front of her. Knowing that she didn't need to fear him on a physical level in no way reassured Abby right at the moment. Torr Latimer had a temper, even if he was in control of it.

"That's your whole problem, Abby Lyndon. You don't think things through, you just act. You're a creature of impulse. You let your lack of self-discipline lead you into all sorts of dangerous situations. If some man doesn't take charge of you, you're going to find yourself in quicksand one of these days."

"You don't have to yell at me as if I were a stupid little child." She felt obliged to defend herself.

"I know full well you're no child," he exploded. "That's the whole problem. You're a woman and you need a man to keep you out of mischief. It's becoming obvious that your lack of foresight and restraint are going to land you in trouble."

"That's hardly fair, Torr," she protested indignantly. "I've survived up till now."

"Barely!"

"You're overstating the problem," she returned aloofly.

"It would be impossible to overstate the problem. I knew from the first moment I saw you in class that you had a nasty tendency to follow your undisciplined impulses."

"You used to think it was a cute habit, not a nasty one," she reminded him. "I believe you called me adventurous."

"Don't think you're going to get out of this by distracting me."

"Nothing could distract you, Torr," she grumbled. "I may be undisciplined, impulsive and reckless but you're just the opposite, aren't you? It's amazing you can even tolerate me."

"And don't think you're going to escape by pulling that pathetic little scatterbrained routine," he warned.

"Escape what?" she inquired interestedly. "Are you going to beat me?"

"Don't tempt me."

"It might be interesting to see you do something rash and impulsive," she mused.

Torr's lashes came down, narrowing his amber gaze rather dangerously. "Abby, at the moment you are skating on very thin ice. The only reason I'm not whaling the daylights out of you right now is because you've already been through enough violence for one evening."

"That," she declared easily, "was quite different." She took a sip of wine as Torr stared at her. Then she smiled gently. "You don't have to worry that I'd ever confuse your temper with Flynn's sick viciousness."

Torr inhaled deliberately, his hands on his hips. "How is it," he asked grimly, "that you know instinctively how to disarm me?"

"Have I disarmed you, Torr?" she whispered, eyes gleaming with the warmth of her emotions. She loved this man, even when he was yelling at her. She would always love him.

"You're a dangerous woman, Abby Lyndon. Somehow I've got to discover a way to get the upper hand in this relationship or I'll find myself riding the tiger," he groaned just as the telephone rang. As if he was grateful for the interruption, Torr grabbed up the receiver.

"Hello? Oh, it's you, Tyson. Abby and I were going to call you later. After I finish tearing a strip off her, that is. Mad? You're right, I'm mad. Not that it's doing me much good. The woman is a menace. She ought to be chained to the kitchen sink on a leash that's just long enough to reach to the bedroom. I plan to invest in some sturdy chains. What? Yes, I figure you probably had a reason for calling. Who goes first?"

Abby sipped her wine and pretended to ignore Torr's glare as he stood listening to Ward.

"When did you find out? That's just what we were going to call and tell you. Randolph showed up here around six o'clock. I wasn't in the apartment at the time and Abby had strict instruction not to open the door." There was a pause and then Torr went on gruffly, "How did you guess? She opened it all right and found herself fighting him off. The man's over the edge, Tyson. Nuttier than a fruitcake but a lot more dangerous. I think seeing Abby face-to-face again and finding out she wasn't going to let him have his revenge finally pushed him over the brink. He's in custody down at the psychiatric ward in the hospital. Police took him away a couple of hours ago and booked him for assault, among other things. Oh, Abby? She's okay. By the skin of her teeth. When I walked in she was in the process of cracking a flower bowl over Randolph's head. But that's typical of Abby. Never could resist messing up a perfectly satisfactory flower arrangement."

Abby sniffed disdainfully as Torr paused to listen again. He sent her a silencing glance.

"Right," he continued a moment later into the phone. "He was the one behind the blackmail. He's also the one trying to buy up those shares. That's what he was going to blackmail Abby for, by the way. Oh, I see." Torr nodded, frowning thoughtfully. "Right. That's that, then. What? Of course, I'm going to marry her. What else can I do? I was trying to give her some time. Trying to respect her sensitive, fragile, delicate female feelings and not rush her, but I can see that it's only inviting disaster to wait. The woman needs a husband to keep her in line and I wouldn't want to wish the job on anybody else. So her sensitive, delicate, fragile female feelings are just going to have to adjust to the situation a little sooner than planned, that's all. Besides, any woman who's capable of cracking a bowl over a man's head obviously can take care of her fragile feelings. Fine. I'll talk to you later. Good night, Tyson."

Torr hung up the phone and glowered at Abby who was staring at him with all the wonder and hope she was feeling reflected in her blue eyes. "Ward just found out from the investigator that Randolph was the one who approached the relatives about buying up their shares. The investigator suggested a link between that action and the threat against you when he found out you owned a sizable chunk of those shares. Too bad that high-priced investigator didn't come up with that conclusion this morning instead of this afternoon. Could have saved us all a lot of trouble."

"Torr, did you mean it?" Abby broke in to ask.

"Of course I meant it. You think it's pleasant to walk in and find your woman being assaulted by another man? You think I want to make a practice of that kind of thing? Abby, if you ever do that to me again I'll lock you up and throw away the key. Where was I? Oh, yes. Ward also said that the investigator concluded that Randolph is nuts. A little late with that analysis, too, if you ask me. Apparently about six months ago Randolph lost his position as vice president of that real estate firm he was with. Got a reputation for being unreliable and erratic on the job. The trauma of being fired was what probably pushed him far enough to start thinking of revenge. Tomorrow I'll phone Tyson back and see if he's got any idea who in his firm might have sold information to Randolph. Randolph must have been bribing someone to tip him off about the progress of the company."

"He was. He said he had a pipeline into Ward's firm." Abby brushed that problem aside in her haste to get to the main issue at hand. "Did you mean what you said about marrying me?" She got to her feet, holding the ends of her bathrobe sash in both hands. Urgently she regarded him. Her honeyed hair was knotted in a loose, tousled bun and the robe was rather ancient. She undoubtedly did not look at all as a woman should look when she was receiving a proposal of marriage but, then, this was hardly a normal sort of proposal.

Torr eyed her narrowly. "I never say anything I don't mean. I'm going to marry you all right. I was going to give you time to get used to the idea of living with me, but I have decided that more stringent steps are required. I'm going to tie you to me so thoroughly you won't ever be able to run. I realize that sort of possessiveness undoubtedly offends your finer sensibilities," he mocked roughly, "but as far as I'm concerned you had your chance to do this slowly and you blew it. If you can't be trusted to obey a lover then we'll see how well you can learn to obey a husband. And I'm warning you, Abby Lyndon, husbands are not to be trifled with. Husbands aren't like lovers who have to be gallant and gentlemanly all the time. Husbands have a lot of rights lovers can't claim."

"You seem to know a lot about the subject."

Torr stepped toward her and sank his fingers into her shoulders, his amber eyes almost golden with the intensity of his words. "I know exactly what kind of husband I will make, Abby. I'm going to be demanding and possessive and overbearing and possibly even downright domineering at times. But I will love you for as long as I live and that, my wary little wife-to-be, will make all the difference."

She smiled tremulously up at him, knowing he spoke the truth. "Yes, with you that makes all the difference."

Torr's expression of grim determination warmed into softer emotion. "Abby?"

"I love you, Torr. You know that."

He appeared to have difficulty collecting his words. "No. I didn't know that. Not for certain. How could I have known?"

"You told me that second time we made love that you thought I could be controlled with love."

"I meant my love for you," he groaned. "I didn't realize at the time that you loved me."

Abby reached up to touch his cheek. "And here I thought you understood me so well because you could seduce me so easily. I decided you must have known exactly how far I'd fallen."

He shook his head. "When I asked you to come and live with me, you almost refused," he reminded her.

"Only because I wasn't certain of your feelings. I wanted a commitment, and it took me a while to realize that you had already made one. Oh, Torr, do you really love me?"

"I think I must have fallen in love with you the first night of class," he murmured as he pulled her close.

"Everything you did fascinated me. I could have spent the entire class just watching you create your wild flower arrangements. Mine always seemed so stark and uninteresting by comparison."

Abby laughed softly. "Yours always seemed so elegant and strong. Anything but stark and uninteresting and you know it. I still think you should enter that competition Mrs. Yamamoto told you about."

"We'll talk about that later. Right now all I want to discuss is you and me. Abby, honey, put me out of my misery and tell me how long you've known you loved me?" He crushed her warmly against his chest, his cheek resting on her hair as she willingly snuggled close.

"I've been sure for several days. I fell in love with you sometime during the days we spent at the cabin. Probably before that. It was just that during that time at the cabin I knew for certain."

"Why didn't you tell me?" he ground out, sounding both vastly relieved and vastly annoyed. "If you knew what I've been going through trying not to scare you off . . ."

"I wasn't sure how you felt about me," she admitted. "I thought when you asked me to live with you rather than marry you it meant you weren't sure yet of your own feelings. I was going to give you time. All the time it took to make you fall in love with me."

"With both of us bent on giving each other time we're lucky the whole problem got resolved so quickly. I'm warning you now, though, that you'd better not make a habit out of creating a crisis whenever you want something resolved."

"Yes, Torr."

He grinned with sudden wickedness. "You're learning. Just keep saying 'yes, Torr' and we'll have a nice long, placid marriage."

"Placid?"

"Ummm. You know me. Reserved, quiet, placid." He turned her halfway around in the curve of his arm and gently began undoing the sash of the robe.

"Reserved, quiet and placid," Abby repeated thoughtfully, leaning back against him. "Sounds wonderful."

"Actually, knowing you, it sounds impossible. I have a feeling my life is in for something of a change." He slipped the robe off her shoulders, letting it fall to the floor at her feet. His fingers toyed with the prim, crocheted collar of the flannel nightgown she wore.

"Will you mind?" she asked as she turned to face him.

"The only thing I could possibly mind is losing you for any reason. Abby, honey, you're the most important thing in my life. I'm not even sure there was anything at all important in my life, in fact, until you came along."

Abby looked up at him through her lashes as she carefully, methodically undid the bodice of the nightgown. "Are you going to make love to me instead of finishing the lecture?"

"Would finishing the lecture do any good?"

"Not nearly as much good as making love to me," she assured him lovingly. Her fingers curled up around his neck.

"That's what I decided, too." He lifted her up into his arms as the nightgown fell away. "Sweetheart, I'm going to take you to bed and make love to you all night long. I need you so much."

"I think you are going to prove more manageable than you realize," she teased throatily, aware of the exciting roughness of his chest hair against her bare breast.

He started toward the hall with her in his arms and his amber eyes gleamed down at her. "If this is your management technique, feel free to pursue it at any time."

"The only problem with it is that I'm not sure which of us is managing the other," she sighed.

"Just remember that I'm the one who always got praised in flower-arranging class." He paused by the kitchen counter, balancing her precariously for a moment as he reached toward the vase of erratically arranged flowers Abby had put together earlier in the evening. Carefully he chose one of the orchids and dropped it on her bare stomach.

Without a word he continued down the hall and into her bedroom, settling his burden in the center of the turned-back sheets. Aching with love, Abby watched him undress, the sight of his strong solid body creating an unbearable excitement in her.

"You're just like one of your own flower arrangements," she breathed as he came down beside her. "Strong and sure and incredibly masculine."

He laughed huskily as he lazily reached out to adjust the orchid between her breasts. "I wonder how many women would see a man in terms of flowers." He lowered his dark head and kissed the peaking tip of one gentle globe.

"For the record, Torr Latimer, let me make it clear that I don't want any other woman seeing you the way I see you," Abby declared with surprising fierceness as she fit her palm to the muscular planes of his thigh.

"That sounds suspiciously possessive to me."

"It does, doesn't it?" Abby wasn't particularly concerned by the fact and it showed. She drew her fingertips up along the inside of Torr's leg with slow, tantalizing movements that elicited a heavy groan from him.

"Does that mean I'm not going to have to walk on eggs around you in the future? No more having to be cautious about offending you or scaring you or making you withdraw?" He shifted slightly, inserting his leg aggressively between hers.

"Since when have you ever had to walk on eggs around me?" Abby let her head fall back on his arm, challenging him with love and laughter in her eyes.

"I'll have you know I've been exceedingly careful right from the start. You can't possibly know what a strain it's been," he rasped.

"And to think I never realized," she murmured wonderingly.

"There are a lot of things you never realized. But I intend to bring each and every one of them to your attention during the next sixty or seventy years."

"You're going to teach me to control my impulsive, undisciplined approach to life?"

"No. I figure that's an impossible task. I'll just have to be content with showing you all of the infinite number of ways there are to arrange flowers."

Abby pulled his head down to hers and the orchid between her breasts was fragrantly crushed as Torr took loving possession of his woman.

New York Times Bestselling Author

CHARLOTTE VALE ALLEN

Three women, three haunted pasts.

DREAMING IN COLOR

Bobby Salton is a woman on the run. With her young daughter, she finds refuge in a rambling house on the Connecticut shore. Alma Ogilvie is a retired head mistress, who, with Bobby's help, wants to regain the independence she lost following a stroke. Eva Rule, Alma's niece, is a successful writer who is trying desperately to put the past behind her—until Bobby shows up.

Now as they all begin to hope for the future, will past threats ruin everything?

Watch for *Dreaming in Color*, this April at your favorite retail outlet.

MILLION DOLLAR SWEEPSTAKES (III)

This April, Harlequin and Silhouette
are proud to bring you

Just
Add
Children

How do you guarantee a lively romance? Take a
handsome, single man and a successful, single woman—
then...*Just Add Children.*

Three complete novels by your favorite authors—
in one special collection!

BABY, IT'S YOU by Elise Title
NATURAL TOUCH by Cathy Gillen Thacker
TO LOVE THEM ALL by Eva Rutland

Available wherever
Harlequin and Silhouette books are sold.

HREQ495

Harlequin invites you to the most
romantic wedding of the season.

Rope the cowboy of your dreams in
Marry Me, Cowboy!

A collection of 4 brand-new stories,
celebrating weddings, written by:

New York Times bestselling author

JANET DAILEY

and favorite authors

Margaret Way
Anne McAllister
Susan Fox

Be sure not to miss Marry Me, Cowboy!
coming this April

 HARLEQUIN ®

MMC

Bestselling Author

Janice Kaiser

Look in on the secret lives and loves of a powerful family in

Private SINS

Brett— the brilliant young attorney who dares to fall in love with her husband's son.

Amory—a supreme court judge who will have to put his heart and life on the line.

Elliot—a man trapped by his contempt for his wife and his forbidden love for his father's bride.

Monica—the bitter wife who will make her husband pay for daring to love another.

Harrison—a senator whose scandalous affairs may cost him more than his career.

Megan—the senator's aide and mistress, whose dreams may be on the cutting block.

Get to know them intimately this March,
at your favorite retail outlet.

MIRA The brightest star in women's fiction

MJKPS

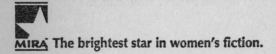